# & Choices

...*Plus!*

**ARE YOU A REAL GO-GETTER?**
TRY OUR FAB QUIZ AT
THE BACK OF THE BOOK

SOME SECRETS ARE JUST TOO GOOD TO KEEP
TO YOURSELF!

**Sugar Secrets...**

# Sugar
## SECRETS...

### ...& Choices

## Mel Sparke

## Collins
*An Imprint of HarperCollinsPublishers*

Published in Great Britain by Collins in 1999
Collins is an imprint of HarperCollins*Publishers* Ltd
77–85 Fulham Palace Road, Hammersmith, London W6 8JB

The HarperCollins website address is
www.**fire**and**water**.com

9 8 7 6 5 4 3 2 1

Creative consultant: Sue Dando
Copyright © Sugar 1999. Licensed with TLC

ISBN 0 00 675436 8

Printed and bound in Great Britain by
Caledonian International Book Manufacturing Ltd, Glasgow

Conditions of Sale

This book is sold subject to the condition that it shall not, by way of trade
or otherwise, be lent, re-sold, hired out or otherwise circulated without
the publisher's prior consent in any form of binding or cover other than
that in which it is published and without a similar condition including this
condition being imposed on the subsequent purchaser.

# CHAPTER 1

●●●●●●●●●●●●●●●●●●●●●●●●●●●

## THE ARGUMENT

"Kerr-rry... Kerrr-RRY... KERRRRRY!!!"

Kerry Bellamy thumped the novel she was reading down on to the sofa and stood up for what seemed like the twentieth time.

"What?" she snapped. "What is it *now*, Lewis?"

Stomping into the hallway she stood at the bottom of the stairs and glared up at her six-year-old brother. Lewis was standing on the top stair in his Spider-Man pyjamas, his beloved Eeyore toy dangling from one hand.

"I'm thirsty," he whined.

"Well, go and get a drink of water then," ordered Kerry. "You know where the bathroom is."

"*Can't*," he whimpered, "I haven't got a glass."

Huffing dramatically, Kerry turned and made her way to the kitchen.

"Go back to bed, Lewis, and I'll bring you one up," she shouted over her shoulder. It was the third time her brother had called out to her from his bedroom in the last hour and Kerry was becoming increasingly irritated as the evening went on.

*It's bad enough having to be stuck indoors babysitting on a Saturday night,* she thought, *but when your darned little brother starts playing you up too...*

Kerry filled a glass with water and trudged upstairs to Lewis's room. He was sitting on his bed looking so doleful that Kerry felt slightly guilty for being so cross. She handed over the glass and sat down next to him.

Lewis drained the water in seconds and thrust the glass into her lap.

"Kerry?"

"Yes, Lewis."

"Why are you in a bad mood?"

"Because you should be asleep and you're not," Kerry answered testily. "Instead, you're being really annoying and driving me mad."

Lewis frowned slightly. "But you were in a bad mood before I went to bed, Kerry. You've been in a bad mood all day."

Kerry motioned for Lewis to get into bed and helped snuggle him down under his Star Wars duvet cover. She could never be cross with her adorable little brother for long.

"Well, if you promise to go to sleep now, then I promise I'll be more cheerful tomorrow," she said more gently, brushing away a few stray strands of hair from his eyes. "Deal?"

"OK," said Lewis, closing his eyes and hugging Eeyore.

Kerry stood up and made her way out of the room.

"Night, Kerry."

"Goodnight, Lewis – sleep tight."

Of course, Lewis was right, Kerry realised as she slouched back down to the living room. She was in a bad mood and had been all day. And she knew exactly why. It was all because of Ollie and the petty row they'd had yesterday over which film they were going to see at the weekend. Ollie had plumped for the latest Hollywood action movie, while Kerry had set her heart on a slushy comedy.

Neither would budge and the phone conversation had ended with Ollie declaring that he would go to the pictures with Joe instead, and Kerry muttering a barely audible "Bye then" before slamming the phone down.

But more than that, Kerry knew that the row hadn't been an isolated incident. She and Ollie seemed to keep on bickering recently, generally over some minor issue. The thing was, Kerry knew that it disguised a much bigger problem: the real problem that she didn't know how to resolve.

She and Ollie had been going out for quite a while now and their relationship had been so good. Recently, although nothing had been said, Kerry got the feeling that Ollie wanted to take things further.

So far they'd only kissed and cuddled, and Kerry felt comfortable with that...

No longer able to concentrate on her book, Kerry switched on the television, but after flicking idly through the channels, she turned it off. Her thoughts were entirely on herself and Ollie.

*The trouble is, I've had no real experience of boys, but Ollie has been out with other girls – take Elaine, for instance. Surely he'll get fed up with just kissing soon and want more. After all, he's bound to have more experience than me.*

Kerry knew that she had blown the whole thing out of all proportion and now it frightened her half to death.

*Why can't we just stay as we are?* she thought bleakly. *Why does he want more from me than I'm ready to give?*

Kerry's thoughts were interrupted by a knock at the front door. She knew instantly that it was Ollie: he rapped out the same little tune with his knuckles every time he called on her at home.

Surprised, she went to open the door.

Ollie Stanton stood on the doorstep with a cute, fluffy toy rabbit in his hand and a look of uncertainty on his face.

"Peace offering," he said simply as she threw her arms round his neck and hugged him, flattening the rabbit between them.

"Oh, Ollie, I'm so sorry we rowed!" cried Kerry, her grumpy mood dissolving instantly. "It's all my fault, I was just being a cow."

"No, really, it was me," countered Ollie. "I should have gone along with your suggestion – I wanted to see that film anyway. Can we pretend it never happened?"

Unpeeling herself from him, Kerry smiled and nodded. "Are you coming inside?"

"I thought you'd never ask," grinned Ollie, handing her the bunny and stepping into the house.

"Thanks, he's so cute," Kerry said. "I'll take him to b..." Then realising what she was about to say, she blushed deeply. "I'll put him on my windowsill with the others," she corrected herself quickly. "D'you want a coffee?"

"Mmm, please." Ollie followed Kerry to the kitchen and plonked himself easily on the table, his legs dangling over the side. "Lewis in bed?"

"Sort of," Kerry answered, filling the kettle with water. "He's been up three times though. So you knew I'd been roped into babysitting?"

"Mmm. Sonja told me this morning. I called you a couple of times today, but there was no reply."

Kerry peered sheepishly at Ollie as she took the coffee jar from the cupboard.

"Everyone's been out except me," she explained, "and I've been feeling so miserable I couldn't even be bothered to answer the phone. Sorry."

Ollie was desperate to ask what it was that had been making her so unhappy recently, but he didn't feel it was the right time. Instead, he just smiled sympathetically and said nothing.

"So you decided not to go to the pictures with Joe after all?" Kerry carried on brightly.

"Nah, I didn't fancy it in the end. And when I heard you were in on your own all evening I decided to come round and try and make amends."

"That's sweet," Kerry flushed. "You really know how to make me feel bad for not making the first move."

"Sorry," he grinned. "It wasn't intended. So what are your parents up to this evening?"

"Oh, some 40th birthday party somewhere. They had a babysitter planned but she called up and said she was sick. So, as I wasn't doing anything, I was hauled in off the subs' bench." Kerry made a face. "I would have been having quite a nice time on my own with my book except for Lewis insisting on annoying me when he should be in bed."

"And then me turning up unannounced..." added Ollie wryly.

"Oh, no, Ol, I didn't mean it like that!" Kerry exclaimed. "I'm really glad you came round."

"Good," he said. "Anyway talking of being on your own, Nick's going away in a week or so and he's asked me to flat-sit for him. Isn't that great?"

"Yeah, I guess..." Kerry couldn't see the attraction herself. Ollie's Uncle Nick lived above his second-hand record shop, Nick's Slick Riffs. If the shop was anything to go by, the flat was probably quite sleazy.

"I mean, much as I get on with Mum and Dad it'll be fab to have my own space, even if it's just for ten days," Ollie continued. "It'll be good for us too. Give us somewhere to hang out together without any interruptions from parents or the others..."

Kerry suddenly thought she realised what Ollie was getting at. She turned abruptly from the coffee things she was sorting and stared hard at him. "What do you mean?"

Ollie looked blankly back. "Um, well, I just think it'll be nice for us to spend some time on our own. I could cook my special spag bol for you. Or we could just, y'know, hang out, watch videos. Be together – like a proper couple."

Kerry felt the tension rise in her body. What did he mean, "spend some time on our own, like a proper couple"? Was he proposing they spend the night together at Nick's? Kerry was indignant.

"What exactly are you saying, Ollie?" she asked accusingly.

Ollie looked completely flummoxed. "Nothing, Kez. Look, it's just an idea. You don't have to come round if you don't want to. I thought it would be... fun."

From the frosty look on her face, Ollie could see that Kerry considered this idea anything but fun.

*What on earth's wrong with her?* he thought. *Anyone would think I just asked her to stick needles in her eyes.*

He cast around for something else to say but Kerry didn't give him the chance.

"I thought we did have fun, Ollie," she said,

feeling angry and fearful at the same time. "I didn't realise you thought I'd become boring..." She broke off and fought back the tears that were pricking the backs of her eyes. She wanted to add ...*because I'm not ready to sleep with you*, but she just couldn't bring herself to say it.

"Jesus, Kez!" said Ollie in exasperation. "What is it with you? It's like you're just looking to pick a fight all the time. I don't get what's got into you."

"It's not me you should be looking at," Kerry said, her chin wobbling. "I'm not the one who's changed. I'm not the one who wants things to be different..." She broke off again, frightened by what she might say next, scared of bringing her real feelings out into the open.

"What do you mean, Kez?" Ollie was completely baffled by the outburst.

"Look," she replied, unable to explain herself any further, "I think you'd better go." She turned away from him and began fiddling with the coffee things.

Ollie let out a "Pttptt!" of annoyance and shook his head.

"I don't know what's got into you, Kerry," he said quietly, jumping off the table and retreating towards the hallway. "I thought we had something special. Maybe I was wrong."

He opened the door and left the house, pulling the door closed with a clatter.

Kerry threw the spoon she'd been fiddling with down on to the work surface and burst into tears.

# CHAPTER 2

● ● ● ● ● ● ● ● ● ● ● ● ● ● ● ● ● ● ● ● ● ● ● ● ● ● ● ● ● ● ●

## KERRY'S DILEMMA

When Joe Gladwin walked into the End-of-the-Line café on Sunday morning and saw Maya sitting by herself at the gang's usual table, he was tempted to turn around and walk back out again. He would have done, if she hadn't looked up from her Coke, given him a broad smile and mouthed "Hello".

The truth was, Joe had been steering clear of Maya Joshi since their end-of-summer day-trip to the beach at Maiden Bay. It had been a day of real torment for Joe because Kerry and Ollie had fallen out. And while Joe had held Kerry in his arms to comfort her, the all-seeing Maya had discovered his biggest secret – that he was desperately, hopelessly in love with Kerry himself.

The fact that Maya had realised this terrified

him – he couldn't bear the thought of anyone knowing his true feelings. Joe trusted Maya to keep the knowledge to herself, but he felt sure that Maya would try to talk to him about it and he didn't want that. Hence his avoidance tactics.

They'd worked quite nicely – until now.

Joe walked reluctantly over to Maya, a smile frozen on his face and a fearful voice in his head shouting, *Get me out of here!*

"Hi, Maya," he managed to croak.

"Come and sit down," said Maya. "I wondered how much longer I was going to have to sit here by myself. The others must all be having a lie-in."

Joe shuffled his feet uneasily. "I'll just go and get a drink," he said, looking at her half-empty glass. "D'you want another Coke?"

Maya shook her head and Joe retreated gratefully to the counter. He ordered a coffee from Anna and stood waiting while she made it instead of wandering back and sitting down as he'd normally do. He desperately hoped one of the others would walk in so that he would be spared the agonies of having to talk to Maya. But, less than a minute later, he was forced to take his drink and rejoin her at the window seat.

"So, Joe," she said, "I feel like I haven't seen you for days. What have you been up to?"

"Well, uh, I..." he mumbled, before trailing

off. Joe's mind had gone blank, as it invariably did when he felt under pressure.

"Has much been happening with The Loud?" encouraged Maya.

"Oh, right," Joe brightened. He could chat quite easily about the band that he, Ollie and Billy were in without getting too tongue-tied.

"It's finally going great. We're getting together this evening at Ollie's to decide on some songs to rehearse. And we need to talk about who the fourth band member is going to be."

"So Billy's a permanent fixture with you and Ollie then?" asked Maya.

"Oh, yeah!" said Joe eagerly. "He's great, really enthusiastic and a good guitarist."

Maya felt her skin prickle with irritation. She still didn't like the idea of Billy Sanderson being around so much; after all, she'd introduced him to the rest of the crowd. But she couldn't work out *why* it bothered her, which bugged her even more.

She fleetingly wondered whether to talk to Joe of her feelings, then decided against it. There was something she wanted to ask him which was far more pressing.

She was acutely aware that Joe had been keeping out of her way and she knew why. Maya had seen the way he'd looked at Kerry that day at Maiden Bay, and the way he'd held her when she'd been upset over that argument with Ollie.

Although he'd said nothing, Maya's intuition had told her that Joe was in love with Kerry and she knew it must be tearing him apart. Maybe now was her chance to talk to him about it.

"Joe?"

"Uh-huh?"

"You remember that day at the beach...?"

Joe's heart lurched and his mouth went dry. *Of course, how could I forget?* he thought. *Darn! I knew you'd want to talk about it.* He took a slug of coffee and nodded reluctantly.

Knowing how reticent Joe could be, Maya didn't quite know how to broach the subject of their friend. But she was keen to reassure him that she hadn't told anyone his secret.

She formulated the words carefully in her head before speaking.

"I just... well, I just wanted you to know that I really won't say anything to the others about, you know, Kerry... and I wanted to make sure you were OK about it all."

Joe felt his face flush. His heart missed a beat, or several. He gulped.

*I really don't want to discuss this,* the voice in his head screamed, *but how do I get out of it?*

Joe suddenly decided on the best line of defence.

"Sorry?" he said, his eyebrows knitted together

in consternation. "I... er, I'm not sure I know what you're getting at."

Maya realised immediately that Joe wasn't ready to talk; he'd never admitted being in love with Kerry when she'd told him she knew, and had obviously decided to deny it now. She sorely wished she had never brought the subject up.

It was a huge relief to both of them to spot Sonja and Kerry walking towards the café.

"Uh, look, it doesn't matter," she said quickly, waving through the window at them. "Maybe we can talk another time."

Joe flushed again as Kerry came towards the table. He felt he was under attack from all angles and was desperate to escape.

Sonja Harvey breezed into the café and plonked herself down next to Maya, while Kerry stood at the end of the table looking thoroughly miserable.

"Kerry, you look terrible. What's up?" exclaimed Maya.

"Sit down and calm down while I get the coffees in," Sonja instructed Kerry. "Then you can tell Maya all about it."

Joe felt a wave of panic rising inside him. He knew he had to get out of there. When his love for Kerry had been his secret alone, he could have coped with a situation like this – just. Now he knew that Maya would be watching his reactions like a hawk, he suddenly realised he couldn't handle it.

Pushing his coffee cup away, Joe stood up.

"I, uh... sorry to butt out like this," he spluttered, "but I've just remembered there's something I have to do right now. I'll see you guys later."

Then he bolted for the door.

"What's up with Joe?" said Kerry, watching his rapidly retreating frame disappear into the street.

"I'm not sure," Maya replied. "I think he's got a lot on his mind. Anyway," she said, keen to change the subject, "what's happened to you?"

Sonja went to order the coffees while Kerry slumped into the seat Joe had vacated and hunched over the table. She had already given Sonja a brief run-through of last night's events on the way to the café, but she was grateful to retell her story to Maya.

"It's me and Ollie," she said. "We had a row last night and I told him to leave. I think we're going to split up..."

Maya looked shocked. "Kerry, are you sure? What's happened?"

"Oh, Maya, it was horrible!" sobbed Kerry. "We had a row on Friday over which stupid film we were going to see and I put the phone down on him. So, last night, Ollie came round and he was really sweet and then– and then..."

Kerry's voice broke and she looked down at the coffee cup Sonja had placed in front of her. Maya reached over and touched her arm gently.

"Go on," she encouraged.

"Everything was fine," continued Kerry, "until Ollie started going on about him flat-sitting for Nick when Nick goes away next week. He was saying how great it would be for us to have somewhere to be alone together, how we'd be like a proper couple... and I just felt like he was getting at... you know, like he was suggesting we spend the night together. And I flipped. I told him to leave, and he did. I've spent the whole night worrying about it."

"You poor thing," Maya sympathised. "You look like you haven't slept at all."

"I haven't. Things haven't been brilliant between us recently, but we've *never* rowed like that before," sniffed Kerry. "It just makes me realise how wrong it feels between us now. And the worst thing is, I can't see any way of getting us back to how we were."

Kerry took a sip of her coffee and blinked away the tears welling up in her eyes. "I don't know, I thought we were right for each other. Now I'm not so sure... and Ollie said as much when he left last night."

Maya thought she knew what was on Kerry's mind. She had been in such a state on that trip to Maiden Bay. Maya remembered the way Kerry had clung to Joe while confessing to Maya that she was feeling under pressure to have sex with Ollie.

"Kerry," said Maya, squeezing her friend's hand, "you still haven't talked to Ollie about all this, have you?"

Kerry shook her head dolefully and took another sip of coffee.

"Do you know for sure that Ollie wants you to sleep together?"

"No," squeaked Kerry.

"Then could it be that you're both getting your wires crossed here?"

"Uh... I guess so."

"So," Maya continued, "the big question, Kez, is *why* haven't you spoken to Ollie about it yet? I thought you were going to talk to him at the beach. What happened?"

Kerry looked up at the ceiling as if searching for inspiration.

"I don't know," she said finally. "It's such a hard subject to talk about in a *casual* way. I did try to talk to Ollie that afternoon, but then I chickened out. I mean, it's not the sort of thing that comes up in conversation, is it? And I guess I feel embarrassed because I've never spoken to anyone about that sort of stuff before. Not like this, anyway."

"So, in the mean time," said Sonja, "you're getting more and more uptight because you *think* he wants to have sex with you, even though you don't *know* that's the case. And you're jeopardising what might be the most wonderful relationship of your life because you feel you can't talk to him about it?"

"I know," Kerry answered flatly. "It's stupid and immature and I've got a real hang-up about it. I keep thinking I've already ruined everything by pushing him away and picking arguments all the time."

"No, you haven't, Kez," said Maya gently. "Ollie cares too much about you to let you go that easily. But nothing will be resolved unless you talk to him, however difficult that might be. You've got to do it, Kerry, and the sooner the better. Don't you see?"

"Yes," Kerry answered in a small voice...

# CHAPTER 3

● ● ● ● ● ● ● ● ● ● ● ● ● ● ● ● ● ● ● ● ● ● ● ● ● ● ● ● ●

## ALL SHOOK UP

Ollie sat on a table in the function room at the back of The Swan and stared despondently out into the semi-darkness beyond. He really wasn't in the mood for this band meeting. If he had been able to catch up with Joe at all today he would have cancelled, but as Joe was nowhere to be found he decided there was little to do other than go ahead with it.

Like Kerry, Ollie had spent a sleepless night worrying about what was going wrong with their relationship. And he'd fought a mental battle with himself all day over whether to call her or not.

So far he'd toughed it out, figuring that of all the rows they'd had recently, he'd made most of the effort to make amends. Which was crazy seeing as, for the most part, he had no idea what he was supposed to have done wrong.

One thing he did know: it was really beginning to drag him down.

When Joe walked in, Ollie could hardly disguise his sombre mood. Least of all to Joe, who was highly sensitive to other people's emotions at all times.

"Hiya, mate." Ollie managed a weak smile that didn't quite reach his eyes. "How're things?"

"Fine," Joe replied. "I've been looking forward to tonight for ages."

He realised immediately that Ollie had the same hollow-eyed look that Kerry had worn earlier in the day.

*What is going on between them?* he wondered.

Part of him had wanted to hang around to find out what had been troubling Kerry in the café this morning, but the conversation with Maya had been bad enough. Then seeing Kerry so soon afterwards had been more than he could bear.

Maybe Ollie would tell him what the problem was. He would have to wait for Ollie to volunteer the information though because, in so many ways, Joe knew he daren't ask.

"Where have you been all day?" Ollie interrupted Joe's thoughts. "I called round a few times, but you weren't in."

"I've been down at the river," replied Joe. "I've got some more songs for us to work on."

Only Ollie knew that Joe wrote the band's new songs; everyone else thought that they were written by Ollie. Joe liked it that way – he couldn't stand the idea of people knowing the innermost feelings which he poured into his songs.

"Was there something you wanted me to bring tonight?" Joe continued. "I wondered about bringing my guitar – do you want me to go and get it?"

"No, nothing like that. I just wanted a chat..." said Ollie.

His voice trailed off as he realised he couldn't tell Joe he was going to cancel the band meeting, not when Joe was so enthusiastic about it.

Joe took Ollie's reply to mean that he wanted to talk about Kerry. He felt he had to say something.

"You look a bit rough," he managed, half-joking. "Have you been out all night?"

"If only," Ollie replied sardonically. "Nah, mate. I wish. Actually," he broke off to rub tired eyes and run his fingers through his hair, "me and Kerry have had a bit of a fight."

"Oh," Joe said. "Bad?"

"Pretty bad. Bad enough for her to chuck me out of her house. And for us not to be speaking, I guess."

"Oh."

So that was why Kerry had looked as grim this morning as Ollie did now. Joe wasn't sure whether or not to mention the scene at the café. Before he had time to consider it, Ollie carried on.

"I wouldn't feel so bad about it if it was the first argument we'd had, but that's all we seem to be doing at the moment. And it's getting me down."

"Of course. It would," sympathised Joe. "So... er, what have you been rowing about?"

"Well, that's just it, Joe," groaned Ollie. "I'm not sure."

"Oh."

"What I mean," Ollie tried to explain, "is that the rows we've had have been over silly things like what time we need to meet to go somewhere. Or, like last night, Kerry bites my head off for no reason whatsoever. It's like she's on a short fuse all the time, waiting for me to say something she disapproves of so she can jump down my throat."

An image of Kerry sobbing in his arms flooded into Joe's mind, as it had done so many times since that day at Maiden Bay. He remembered feeling excruciatingly uncomfortable as Kerry had talked so openly to him and Maya about how scared she was of the sex thing. Joe would never forget the sensations *he'd* felt as she'd wrapped her arms around him for comfort that day.

It suddenly dawned on Joe that sex was probably still the issue between Kerry and Ollie. But how the hell was he, Joe, going to tell his friend this?

He'd felt inadequate at his inability to offer any advice to Kerry before. He ought to be able to help Ollie now, but he had no real experience of girls and he just didn't know where to start.

*I might be able to write a song about it one day*, he thought wryly. But right now, perhaps the best thing he could do was listen. Maybe that was all Ollie needed.

"Mm, I see," he said, hoping to encourage his friend into talking further.

"Shall I tell you what the worst thing is?" said Ollie, looking glumly at Joe.

"What?"

"I keep thinking that maybe Kerry doesn't love me any more."

Joe was stunned. He couldn't imagine Ollie and Kerry not being an item. However much he loved Kerry himself, the thought of his friends splitting up had never been something he'd ever seriously considered.

Nor had he ever dared to think that one day she might be available again.

Joe didn't know how to react. He could see how cut up Ollie was and he'd witnessed Kerry's distress earlier. He hated the idea of either of them being so sad. But at the same time, if Ollie and Kerry did break up, there might – just might – be a glimmer of hope for him and Kerry.

As soon as that idea struck, Joe dismissed it instantly and chided himself for being so insensitive. He felt as though he was betraying Ollie – and Kerry too. How could he think of himself at a time like this?

He vowed to push his own feelings aside and concentrate on helping them put things right.

"What do you mean?" he said at last.

"It's just a hunch," replied Ollie. "It's the way she keeps pushing me away from her, like she doesn't want me anywhere near her. And the nit-picking – why would she be like that if she wasn't fed up with me? I keep thinking that perhaps she hasn't got the guts to dump me, so she's being as horrible as possible in the hope that I finish with her."

"I can't believe it," Joe said emphatically. "Kerry's not like that. She seems to be so completely in love with you – ask anyone. You should have seen her this morning at the End..."

"You've seen her?" Ollie broke in.

"Yeah. She came in with Sonja just as I was... er, leaving. I noticed that she looked... well, pretty much like you do at the moment, Ol. Sort of tired and drained. So my guess is that she's as cut up about your argument as you are."

"Either that or she's upset because I didn't end it there and then," replied Ollie ruefully.

"Have you tried talking to her?" Joe asked.

"She doesn't give me a chance. Take last night. I told her about Nick going away and how I'll be staying in his flat next week. I thought it'd be a good place for us to be on our own, somewhere to talk things through. It would be a great opportunity for us to get that closeness back. But as soon as I even suggested it, Kerry blew a gasket. And I still haven't worked out why. She was ranting on about us not having fun any more, as if she wanted to be out clubbing every night."

"That doesn't sound like Kerry," frowned Joe.

"I know, and that's another reason why I think she's fed up with me. Maybe I'm too boring for her; maybe she wants more excitement, y'know go to clubs, hang out in the City at weekends. Maybe she thinks we're getting too involved, that she's spending too much time with me and not enough time with her mates. I'm not exactly the most exciting guy in the world, am I?"

Joe looked at his friend in total bewilderment. He could hardly believe what he was hearing.

"Surely not, Ol," he said, suddenly lucid. "I mean, we're not talking about a wild child like

Cat here – this is *Kerry*. She's not a die-hard party animal; never has been, never will be. And she adores you, Ol. Everyone knows that. You don't think, er, there might be some misunderstanding between you that could be resolved if you sat down and talked about it?"

This was as much as Joe could bring himself to say about the issue that he was now sure was tearing Kerry and Ollie apart.

Ollie looked at his friend and sighed. "I dunno. Maybe you're right. Maybe we ought to sit down and talk this through."

"It's got to be worth a go, hasn't it?" said Joe, turning away from Ollie as he heard the door open. Billy walked into the room.

"Yeah, you're right, Joe," Ollie smiled for the first time that day. "I'll call her. Tomorrow. Then maybe we can sort this mess out."

# CHAPTER 4

● ● ● ● ● ● ● ● ● ● ● ● ● ● ● ● ● ● ● ● ● ● ● ● ● ●

## KERRY MAKES AMENDS (KIND OF)

Kerry spent the rest of her Sunday striding purposefully to the phone in the Bellamy household, standing over it for a few moments, rehearsing some lines in her head as her hand hovered over the receiver, then skulking guiltily off again. However much she tried, however much she practised their imaginary conversation in her head, she couldn't bring herself to pick up the phone.

Eventually, Kerry convinced herself that it would be far better to see Ollie face to face, rather than confront him on the phone. She decided to call in on him at work on the way home from college next day and felt relief wash over her – albeit temporarily – with the knowledge that she had another twenty-four hours' grace.

Sonja Harvey – being the confrontational sort – badgered Kerry for most of Monday at school.

"Kez, after everything that we discussed yesterday," she'd sighed wearily during lunchbreak, "I can't believe you still haven't spoken to Ollie..."

"I know," Kerry had hissed back. "It's just that my parents were at home all day, so I was limited as to when I could call. And then when I could, I chickened out in case they overheard. I'll do it on the way home from college tonight. I promise."

To make sure that she did, Sonja practically frogmarched Kerry from the college gates to Nick's Slick Riffs where Ollie was working that afternoon.

"The longer you leave it, the harder it will be," said Sonja as she stood outside the café next door. "So I'll be in here waiting for you. Stop by when you've finished and let me know how you got on."

"OK," said Kerry weakly.

She knew Sonja was right. She had to get this sorted once and for all, even though the thought of it made her feel physically sick.

Kerry walked past the poster-clad window of the record shop and opened the door. The musty smell that came from deep within the place hit her immediately, whiffed up her nostrils, rendered her immobile and brought on the biggest, most ungainly sneeze she had ever experienced.

"Aaa-aaa-aaaa-CHOOO!"

Kerry looked up from where she had found herself bent double in the doorway and saw two pairs of startled eyes peering at her in the semi-gloom. Ollie and his Uncle Nick were standing behind the counter and Kerry watched, mortified, as grins as wide as dinner plates spread across their faces.

"Great entrance, Kerry," laughed Nick as he turned and disappeared into the stockroom at the back. "Can you warn me if there's an encore? I'm not sure the old ticker will stand another shock like that."

"Oh... uh... ouff, *sniifff*," Kerry spluttered. She dug into the pockets of her jacket and pulled out a ragged tissue. The opening lines she had planned in her head had deserted her and she was left with the overriding feeling that she looked like a berk.

*Typical,* she thought. *Just when I want to be compos mentis, I end up like a bumbling twerp!*

She took a few steps forward to where Ollie was standing, still grinning.

"Um, hi, Ollie," she said, "sorry about that. I didn't mean to make quite such an entrance..." Her voice trailed off.

"That's OK," he said. "At least you woke us up. We've been catching up on paperwork for most of the afternoon and were on the point of dozing off."

"I, uh... only stopped by to apologise for Saturday night," continued Kerry. "I thought perhaps it was my turn to make the first move."

She stood staring nervously at the till for a moment, unsure of what to say next.

Then she felt Ollie's hand take hold of hers and give it a little squeeze.

"It's OK," he said softly. "It doesn't matter. I was going to call you later anyway."

Kerry felt her heart melt. As she looked into Ollie's all-forgiving face she wondered why she'd been getting so anxious. Ollie was such a decent, caring boyfriend – he would understand once she'd explained to him how she was feeling. All she had to do was tell him...

"I'm sorry, Ol," she said, grasping his hand tightly in hers. "I've been such a misery guts recently and I've been taking it out on you. It's just that there's... there's something I need to talk to you about. It's kind of important."

Kerry looked beyond Ollie to the stockroom behind. She could see Nick's head bobbing up and down between cardboard boxes and knew now wasn't the right time to launch into what she had to say.

"Could we meet up?" she continued. "One evening this week?"

"Sure," Ollie replied. "I'm a bit tied up here tonight, but how about tomorrow night? I should get off at about six. I could meet you next door."

Kerry didn't want to talk to Ollie in the End, not when the others were likely to be in there too. If she was going to tackle the issue that had been tearing her insides out these past few weeks, she needed them to be on their own.

"Uh, I'm not sure," she replied uncertainly. "Perhaps we could meet there, then go on somewhere else. Some place a bit quieter."

"OK," replied Ollie. "Whatever you like. I'll have a think. Maybe we could go and get something to eat in the Plaza."

"That'd be great. Um, how did the band meeting go last night?"

"Brilliant! We all had loads of ideas – it's going to be fab. I can't wait to start rehearsing again—"

"When you've finished, Ollie, could you come back here and give me a hand?" He was interrupted by Nick's voice from the storeroom.

Kerry backed away towards the door. "I'll let you get on," she said. "I'll meet you in the café just after six then."

She turned round, suddenly keen to get out.

"Kerry?" Ollie's voice came from behind her.

She turned back to face him. "Hmmm?"

"Is everything going to be OK?"

"Yes, of course it is. Look, I'll... uh, see you tomorrow."

Kerry returned to Ollie, leaned over the wooden counter and gave him a little kiss on the lips. The corners of her mouth turned up into the ghost of a smile and she left the shop, relieved that at least now she'd set the wheels in motion.

Kerry walked into the End next door, where she saw Sonja, Maya and Cat sitting chatting by the window. Kerry knew Sonja and Maya would be keen to know how she'd just got on and prayed they wouldn't say anything in front of Cat. She really didn't want Cat to know about this.

Much as she liked her, Catrina Osgood could be massively indiscreet and Kerry didn't want the whole of Winstead to know that she was hung up about... sex.

At the sound of the door opening, Sonja looked up.

"Hi, Kez, have you got it sorted?" she asked.

Kerry willed her friend not to say any more, but Sonja had already turned back to Cat to fill her in.

"Kerry's been next door to fix up her next hot date with Ollie," said Sonja brightly, much to Kerry's relief.

"Ah, yes," Cat drawled, "how is love's young dream? Still in the first flush of romance?"

Kerry blushed. *If only you knew,* she thought ruefully.

"Something like that," she replied, then, to change the subject, added, "How's the beauty course going? Have you had a good day?"

"Oh, wow, yes!" enthused Cat. "I did my first facial today. The girl I practised on said I had the most wonderfully supple fingers and a really relaxing action."

"And how about your mum?" Maya asked. "Is *she* more relaxed about you doing this course now?"

Cat wrinkled her nose and gave a long, theatrical sigh. She had been involved in a few unpleasant skirmishes with her mother recently, after Cat had decided to give up her sixth-form place at St Mark's in order to study beauty therapy at Winstead College of Further Education.

The fact that she hadn't let her mum know until after she'd started the course hadn't helped her case much, and relations between the pair had been decidedly frosty ever since.

"Well, she still doesn't approve," Cat explained. "She thinks I should have stayed on to get my A levels and *then* decided on a course. But I think she's beginning to realise that this is what

I really want to do and that I'm happy, and I've offered her loads of free treatments once I know how to do them..."

Breaking off to admire her perfectly made-up nails, freshly painted in Vibrant Blood Orange, Cat looked a little sad, Maya thought.

"To be honest," said Cat, "I keep out of her way most of the time. Who's for another coffee?"

Sliding out of the banquette, Cat stood at the end of the table drumming her nails on the Formica top. "Actually," she added thoughtfully, "I think I'll get something to eat too. Then I can put off going home. Anyone want to share some fries?"

"*That* isn't going to solve anything," said Maya pragmatically. "Wouldn't you be better off making up with your mum rather than hanging around here all night? It's obviously getting you down."

"Honestly, Maya, don't nag," Cat said irritably. "I know what I'm doing. She'll come round, I know she will. Now are you guys going to have something else or do I have to stand here like this all night?"

The others gave their orders and Cat teetered off to the counter in her kitten-heeled boots. Kerry slid into the seat Cat had been occupying and looked shyly at her two friends.

"Well?" Sonja hissed. "What happened? You weren't gone long. Wasn't Ollie there?"

"Oh, he was there," Kerry said, "but so was Nick. So we couldn't talk. We're meeting up tomorrow night so I'll tell him then. I did manage to apologise for flying at him on Saturday night though."

"And?" Maya pressed. "Was he OK about it?"

"He was really sweet – he couldn't have been nicer."

Kerry stared pensively out of the window for a moment. It was starting to get dark and had just begun to rain. Big droplets of water were drizzling down the window pane making the outside world seem a much more depressing place.

"Oh, I really hope we can sort something out," Kerry whispered. "I love him so much, I can't imagine being without him."

## CHAPTER 5

● ● ● ● ● ● ● ● ● ● ● ● ● ● ● ● ● ● ● ● ● ● ● ● ● ● ● ●

### ANYTHING NOT TO TALK

"Aaa-aaaa-aaa-CHOOOO!!!"

Kerry sat at the kitchen table in her dressing gown and pink fluffy socks and just managed to grab a tissue from her pocket before spluttering all over the breakfast things.

"Urgh! YUCKYYUCKYYUCKY!"

Lewis pulled a face from across the table at his sister who was now making a loud, trumpeting sound as she blew her nose. Peering over her wire-rimmed glasses at her younger brother, Kerry saw that he was peering into his bowl with a look of complete horror on his face.

"M-u-m, Kerry got snot in my Krispies!" Lewis complained, turning to Mrs Bellamy who was buttering toast to his left. "I'm not eating them now."

"Don't be silly, Lewis," said his mother. " Of course she didn't. You just concentrate on eating your breakfast or you'll be late for school."

She turned to Kerry who was staring morosely at her own untouched bowl of cereal. "You look terrible, Kerry. I think you ought to go back to bed. It won't hurt you to miss one day of college."

"I feel really grim," sniffed Kerry. "I can't believe this has come on so quickly."

"Colds generally do," said her mother matter-of-factly. "You'll be fine again in a day or so. I'll get you some medicine while I'm out today."

"Thanks, Mum." Kerry stood up gingerly and felt the room spin. She clutched the back of her chair for a few seconds until it stopped. "I'll just phone Sonja to let her know," she said on her way out of the kitchen, "and Ollie 'cause I was supposed to be seeing him tonight."

The first thing Sonja said after "You poor thing, you sound awful" was "You'll do anything to get out of having to talk to Ollie, won't you? Even make yourself ill..."

Sonja was joking, but in a weird way, Kerry knew she had a point. While Kerry was keen to get over this particular hurdle in her relationship with Ollie, she was also relieved that she could put off having to face the issue for a bit longer.

When she'd finished speaking to Sonja, Kerry

picked up the receiver again and dialled the phone number for The Swan.

"Hello?"

"Ollie, hi, it's Kerry. I wasn't sure you'd be up yet."

"Oh, hi, Kez. Yeah, well Nick's asked me to go in early to meet a delivery for the café, so you've just caught me in... Anyway, what are you doing calling me this time of the morning? There's nothing wrong, is there?"

Kerry sneezed into the receiver. "Ooh, sorry," she sniffled. "Actually, I feel terrible. I've got a stinking cold and everything aches, so I don't think I'm going to be able to make it tonight."

"Poor Kez," said Ollie consolingly, "you do sound a bit rough. Don't worry about it, we can make it another time. Are you going to the doctor's?"

"No, I'm going back to bed. I'm sure I'll be fine in a day or two. Could we rearrange a time to go out – maybe Friday evening?"

"Yeah, that'd be great. You sure you'll be OK by then?"

"God, I hope so. I can't imagine it'll last any longer than that."

"OK, if you're sure. Look, I have to go or I'll be late. I'll call you this evening to see how you're getting on. You take care, Kez."

"Thanks, Ol. I'll see you soon."

Kerry put the phone down and dragged her weary body back to bed.

• • •

Anna Michaels wiped her hands on her apron and looked at her watch: 7.55 pm. Only an hour to go before she could shut the café and crawl to her flat upstairs for a sit down. She had been rushed off her feet all day.

She looked out from behind the coffee machine she was cleaning and said "Bye" to a couple of guys who were just leaving. The only people left in the place now were the rowdy gang of Sonja, Cat and Maya at their usual table in the window.

Anna poured herself a coffee and went over to join them.

*I'll just give myself five minutes,* she thought, *then I'll carry on clearing up.*

"Look at this, Anna," Sonja commanded as she approached their table.

Anna watched as Sonja reached over to where Cat was standing at the end of the table and pulled up her shirt. Cat automatically sucked her tummy in and turned to face Anna, who immediately spotted a pink and red tattoo of a

Cupid, complete with bow and arrow, just above Cat's belly button.

"Wow!" gasped Anna. "That's really cool."

"Thank you," Cat answered smugly. "And may I say you have excellent taste, Ms Michaels."

"Yeah, but what do you reckon, Anna?" Sonja cut in. "Fake or real?"

"It's *real*, I told you," protested Cat. "I had it done at the weekend. It took absolutely ages and hurt like hell."

Just then the bell over the door clanked into action and Anna looked guiltily round in case it was Nick coming to check on how things were going. Instead, she was relieved to see Matt Ryan walk through the door.

"Crikey!" Sonja called out. "Hello stranger. What brings you here? It's been so long since we've seen you, we thought you must have emigrated."

Matt grinned. It was true, he hadn't been around the crowd much recently; he'd been spending a lot of time with Gabrielle, his new girlfriend.

"I've been busy," he said by way of explanation. "Anyway, it looks like I've timed it just right, if Cat's about to get her kit off."

Cat wriggled her belly and hitched her shirt just a little bit higher. "Look! Isn't it pretty?" she giggled.

"What is it – a bruise?" joked Matt as he came nearer. "Or a lovebite?"

Cat squealed in false indignation, then twirled a full circle so Matt could get a complete view of her curves.

"What we're trying to work out," Maya explained, "is whether it's real or just a transfer."

"It looks pretty real to me," said Anna.

"I'll tell you if it's fake or not," Matt said, winking at Anna.

He bent down so that his face was only centimetres from the tattoo, then opened his mouth and made as if he was going to lick it. "If it comes off, it's fake," he told Cat. "If not, then we know it's for real."

As he expected, Cat gave out a girlish scream, wriggled out of reach and pulled her shirt down.

"Don't you dare!" she commanded.

"No, I wouldn't," added Sonja. "You might lick her fake tan off too."

Everyone laughed except Cat, who threw a sachet of sugar at her cousin and pretended to sulk.

"So where *have* you been, Matt?" Sonja asked. "I'd forgotten what you looked like."

"Actually, I've been hanging out with Gabrielle," he replied a little sheepishly.

*"Ooo-hh!"* jeered Cat. "Sounds serious. Usually

you're trying to get rid of them by now, not spend time with them. What's the catch?"

"There's no catch," Matt said. "In fact, I think I—"

He stopped short. The depth of his feelings for Gabrielle had taken him by surprise. He'd dated more girls than even he cared to remember, but this thing with Gabrielle was different.

Matt suddenly didn't know what to say. He was dying to announce how he felt to his friends, but didn't know what reaction he'd get. Although there was one thing he could be certain of – Cat would take the mick out of him.

"Go on," Sonja demanded. "You look like El Smugpants as it is, so I know you're dying to tell us something."

Matt shook his head.

"Aw, come on, Matt. I showed you my tattoo, now it's your turn. What do you think? What have you and the lovely Gabrielle been getting up to?" wheedled Cat.

Matt said nothing.

Sonja, determined not to be left out, began to wiggle her fingers. "If you don't tell your Auntie Son what's going on, I'll tickle you until you talk. Are you ready...?"

As Matt knew he would explode soon if he didn't spill the beans, he decided to talk.

"OK, OK! I'm not sure you're going to believe this but what I was going to say was that I really, truly think I'm in love with Gabrielle." He beamed at the four girls, his heart pounding as he made the monumental statement.

"Wha-ttt!" Sonja and Cat squealed in unison. "You? In love? Are you *sure* about this? You're kidding!"

As far as they were concerned, they had never heard anything so ridiculous. The last person on earth they expected to fall in love was Matt, who had a reputation for going through girlfriends with alarming speed.

Matt grinned. "You may mock, but it's true. I've never felt like this about anyone before in my life. What me and Gabrielle have is different, it's special. I can honestly say, hand on heart, that I'm in love with her."

Cat sniggered, while Sonja sat open-mouthed and Anna took a sip of coffee. It was left to Maya to come up with something positive.

"Oh, Matt, that's really sweet," she ventured. "You must be really happy."

"I am," smiled Matt, almost shyly. "It's unbelievable. I never expected it to happen to me. At least, not until I was at least twenty-five and past it."

Anna heard the distant ringing of the café

phone and leapt out of her seat to answer it. "I want to hear all about this, Matt," she said. "So don't say any more until I get back."

She ran into the kitchen and grabbed the phone.

"End-of-the-Line," she said cheerily. "Can I help you?"

"Hello, Anna. How are you?"

Anna's face broke into a grin. She was always pleased to hear from her older brother, Owen. They'd kept in touch by phone nearly every week since he'd finally tracked Anna down to Winstead after she'd run away from home more than a year ago.

"Owen, hi! I'm great, everything's great. How about you? Is the new job still good?"

"Yeah, brilliant. It's hard work, but I'm loving it."

"Good. So what's new?"

"Well, I er... I went to see Mum at the weekend..." he trailed off, waiting for Anna's reaction.

"And?" said Anna flatly.

"And she'd very much like to come down for a day and meet up with you. What do you say?"

Anna didn't answer. She couldn't. Part of the reason why she had left home all those months ago was because she'd become pregnant and her mother had hit the roof. Anna's decision to have an abortion riled the devoutly Catholic Mrs Michaels even more. The rift between them became so great that Anna had walked out one day, not long after she'd come home from hospital. She hadn't had any contact with her mother since.

Although Owen had pleaded with Anna to go some way to rebuilding the relationship, so far she had refused because the pain and anger she felt at being let down so badly by her mum were still too raw for her to deal with.

"I don't know," Anna replied eventually.

It was true. She *didn't* know, and she hated being put on the spot like this. There were a thousand and one emotions rattling through her brain and she simply didn't know what to do for the best.

"Believe me, Anna, I wouldn't suggest this if I didn't think it was going to work out between you," urged Owen earnestly. "Mum is so full of remorse and so devastated by what's happened. She's getting older, she's on her own and she's lonely. She knows she pushed you away and she regrets it so much. She's desperate to make amends. *Please*, Anna!"

Owen was begging and it made Anna feel a little guilty. She loved her brother very much and he'd been terribly upset when he found out what had happened to Anna, and then what had gone on between Anna and her mum. He was doing his best to put things right.

*Can I go through with it?* she thought. *Am I ready for this now? Will I ever be ready...?*

"OK, Owen, you win," she said quickly, before she could change her mind. "I'll see her. But I need you to be here too. I can't face her on my own."

"Oh, Anna, of *course* I will. That's brilliant, really great!" The relief in Owen's voice was obvious. "Thank you – you don't realise what this will mean to her. I'll bring her down. You just name a date and a time and we'll be there."

Anna realised she was shaking as she studied the café shifts diary on the wall in front of her.

"Let's get it over with as soon as possible," she replied. "How about the Saturday after next? I'll call you nearer the time to find out what time your train arrives."

Anna came off the phone feeling as though she'd been run over by a bus. The conversation had dredged up all the hurt of the last couple of years again. She went over to the little sink at the back of the kitchen and splashed her face with cold water.

Determined not to let it get her down, her face took on a steely expression.

*I'm not going to think about this now, I'll think about it when it happens. Perhaps it's for the best. Once we've talked, I can put everything that's happened behind me once and for all.*

She patted her face with a towel and walked back into the café where the others were still larking about. At least there was one person Anna knew would be pleased to hear what was going on.

While Owen had stayed with Anna a few weeks back, he'd had a few dates with Sonja. They had got on so well that, if it wasn't for the fact that Owen now lived far away in Newcastle, Anna was sure that they would now be an item. As she got back to the others, she tapped Sonja on the shoulder and made her announcement.

"Good news, Sonja. That was Owen on the phone. He's coming to visit. The weekend after next."

"Oh, *wow*," Sonja sighed, sinking dramatically back into the red, padded banquette. "I think I've just died and gone to heaven!"

# CHAPTER 6

●●●●●●●●●●●●●●●●●●●●●●●●●●●●●●

## CROSSED WIRES

"Joe, hey, Joe! Hang on! Wait for me!"

Surprised to hear someone calling his name, Joe turned to see Kerry rushing down the road towards him. *Spooky*, he thought, since he'd spent the past half an hour wandering aimlessly through the streets of Winstead, pondering what would happen between Kerry and Ollie. And how anything that happened between them might affect him...

He'd been wondering if they'd sorted out their differences yet or if Kerry had indeed told Ollie she no longer loved him and that was that. Joe hadn't seen much of Ollie all week and when he had, the circumstances hadn't been right for him to bring up the delicate subject of Kerry.

Now it was Friday. Joe had had five days in

which to ponder on what Ollie had said in The Swan. Truth was, he'd thought of little else, and had spent many a restless hour after college sitting in the park or walking by the river or through the town. Just as he was doing now.

Much as he fought against it, deep down Joe thought there was nothing he would like more than for Ollie and Kerry to split up. He'd had many fantasies recently where Kerry fell into his arms and revealed that it was him, not Ollie, that she loved. Joe hated himself for thinking like that, but he just couldn't help it.

Life had been a lot simpler a week ago. In some ways, he'd wished Ollie hadn't confided in him. He loved Kerry from afar, but knew she was out of reach. End of story.

Now, the goalposts had been changed. Now there was the possibility that Ollie and Kerry might end their relationship. What then? Joe knew Ollie would be devastated and yet here he was – Ollie's best friend – secretly rubbing his hands with glee. Some friend!

Even worse, what – if anything – would Joe do about asking Kerry out? She would, after all, be his best friend's ex-girlfriend. Would he be able to stay friends with Ollie if he did that?

Joe doubted it. And he knew how much he needed and valued Ollie's friendship. Ollie was the only person Joe could talk to without feeling like an alien from another planet. Would he seriously risk jeopardising that relationship?

Joe had no answers to the dilemmas whirring around his head. All he knew was that he was in a no-win situation and that thought depressed him.

He tried hard to be cheerful when Kerry caught up with him and started walking alongside.

"Sorry, Kerry, I was miles away," he said, staring hard at the pavement in front of him.

"Where are you off to?" she asked.

"Uh, I dunno really. I was just walking, I guess."

"Oh." Kerry looked quizzically at Joe as if she couldn't understand the idea of anyone wanting to be out "just walking" on a chilly October evening in the middle of Winstead.

"How about you?" he said quickly, hoping it would take her mind off the oddball she was staring at.

"I'm on my way to meet Ollie," she smiled. "We're going for a pizza."

*So everything's all right then*, Joe thought. *You're not splitting up after all.* He wanted to ask her outright but he was too much of a coward. Instead, he let a myriad of emotions at the news – relief, despair, frustration – wash over him.

"Are you going to Robbie Adams' 18th party

tomorrow night?" Kerry asked. She figured Joe would be. The rest of the gang were going, and he and Robbie knew each other quite well. And, as it was being held in the back of The Swan and Joe lived opposite, she guessed there was no reason for him not to.

"Uh... dunno yet. I haven't decided." Joe walked on, staring at the ground.

Kerry realised that Joe was in one of his uncommunicative moods, so she walked next to him in silence. Then, as they turned into the high street, where the Plaza was, Joe announced that he was going the other way, said "Bye" and slunk off.

His actions troubled Kerry. Joe appeared to be nervous and on edge again. This had happened before, but he had been so much more at ease with himself in the past few months.

Now he seemed to be getting weird again and it always appeared to get worse when she was there. But she couldn't work out why.

She would talk to Ollie about it.

And talk they did – about everything other than the sex issue. All the good intentions she'd had when she'd set out that evening went flying out of the restaurant window.

Kerry started by apologising for her grumpiness again. "It's, erm, you know, the wrong time of the month," she said, blushing furiously and fiddling with a breadstick.

"Oh." Ollie looked away. His twin sister, Natasha, had always been pretty open about things like periods, so he was generally able to accept them as a natural part of life. But Kerry's obvious embarrassment was infectious. They'd never talked about anything so intimate before and Ollie wasn't sure what to say next.

Any expression of sympathy – like, "Oh, you poor thing, it must be awful!" – would sound trite. But brushing it under the carpet and changing the subject to the day's weather forecast (which, if he was honest, would be the path he would prefer to take) would be completely heartless.

In the end, Ollie settled for a little squeeze of her hand and what he hoped was a compassionate look. Which made Kerry feel even more guilty for lying.

She didn't even suffer from PMS. Nor, as far as she was aware, did it normally last for several weeks – a fact of which she hoped and prayed that Ollie was ignorant. She squirmed in her seat some more, then changed the subject to something completely innocuous.

Throughout the rest of the meal she willed Ollie to bring up the subject of sex. She almost wished he would come right out and ask her to sleep with him. Then, she thought, she'd be able to deal with it.

At one point, just after they'd ordered their desserts, Ollie looked earnestly at his girlfriend and asked, "Are you happy, Kerry?"

"What?" Kerry said, taken off guard. "What do you mean?"

"With me, I mean," he said. "It's just that I sometimes wonder if you're content to be with me, coming to a place like this for a meal, hanging out in the café. It's not exactly the high life, is it? Occasionally, I wonder if you'd rather be out clubbing, or doing more thrilling things..."

Kerry wrinkled her nose in distaste. "God, no, Ol," she spluttered. "I can't imagine anything worse than being in grotty nightclubs full of slime balls. And as for the way we fill our time, well it suits me just fine. I don't have a problem with that at all."

*So what do you have a problem with then, Kerry?* Ollie was dying to ask. But he didn't have the nerve.

Searching desperately for something else to talk about, Kerry remembered her encounter with Joe earlier.

"I'm a bit worried about Joe," she said. "Have you seen him recently?"

"Not since Sunday night. He seemed fine then. Why, what's happened?"

Kerry related what had gone on between them and added that he had rushed off when she and Sonja had arrived at the café last Sunday morning.

"I dunno, he seems quiet, more so than normal," she explained. "And distant, as though there's something on his mind. You don't think he's drinking again, do you?"

Ollie looked shocked. Joe had hit the booze in a big way earlier on in the year, when he had been depressed about himself and his life. Only Ollie, Kerry and Cat knew about it and, between them, they'd helped Joe overcome his bingeing.

Since then, Ollie thought his friend had been much happier. He had seemed more settled, as if he knew which direction his life was taking now. He seemed excited about The Loud, enthusiastic about sixth form and fitted into the gang much better than before. If there was something serious troubling him again, Ollie didn't know about it.

"I've no idea, Kez," Ollie said, perplexed. "He certainly hasn't shown me any signs that he has."

"It's just a feeling I get. Maybe we ought to keep an eye on him, y'know, make sure he really is OK."

"Yeah, you're right. I'd hate for him to go through all that again."

Ollie took another spoonful of cassata and popped it in his mouth, enjoying the feeling as it melted and slipped down his throat. He studied Kerry while she toyed with her ice cream.

She still looked as though she was weighed down with the worries of ten people. He waited for her to say something else, but it didn't happen. Instead, she chased her ice cream round her plate, eating very little and saying even less.

"Kerry, are you sure that's all?" he said finally. "There's nothing else on your mind?" Ollie was convinced she was hiding something.

"No, of course not. Why should there be?" she replied with a forced lightness in her voice.

"It's just that when you were in the shop the other day, you said there was something important you wanted to talk to me about..."

Kerry felt herself getting flustered. It was no good. She couldn't bring herself to mention sex at all. And she hated herself for being such a coward.

"Uh... it was nothing, Ol. I was more worried about Joe than anything. That's all. Honest."

Ollie let the subject drop. Knowing how short-tempered Kerry'd been recently, the last thing he wanted to do was upset her again. He couldn't face another quarrel.

Ollie felt that an invisible barrier had been put up between them, a brick wall of silence. It was as if they could no longer communicate with each other.

They drank their coffee in silence.

## CHAPTER 7

• • • • • • • • • • • • • • • • • • • • • • • • • •

### FROM BAD TO WORSE

"I wish this party was next week rather than tonight," Sonja complained as she tussled with the zip at the back of her aqua minidress. "I mean, it'd be a great place to go with Owen. As it is, I haven't got anything planned for next weekend."

"Yes, you have," Kerry replied from behind the hand-held mirror she was using to check her face. "It's Maya's birthday on Sunday, remember? We're all going to Pizza Hut."

"Oh, yes, I forgot. It's not the most romantic place to take Owen though, is it?" Sonja grumbled. "An afternoon out in Winstead's finest eatery. That'll really impress him."

Kerry put down the mirror and placed it back in her make-up bag. "Anyway, how do you know he's staying for the weekend? Did Anna tell you that?"

"*Nooo*. She said he's definitely here on Saturday but I'm assuming that once he sees me, he won't *want* to go home." Sonja turned and smirked at Kerry, who raised her eyebrows to the ceiling at her friend's outspoken confidence.

"Right," Sonja carried on, "how do I look?"

She whirled round in her skimpy Lycra dress; she was wearing knee-length black suede boots and her gorgeous blonde hair was piled high on top of her head.

Kerry let out an exaggerated "oooh" of appreciation – Sonja looked absolutely brilliant.

"Fantastic," Kerry sighed. "Swap your body for mine?"

"Don't be silly," Sonja scolded. "You look great too."

Kerry didn't feel great. Instead of being here in Sonja's bedroom, getting ready for Robbie Adams' 18th, she wished she was at home. On her own. She wasn't in the mood for partying, especially seeing as things between her and Ollie now seemed to be worse.

When they'd finished their meal last night, Ollie had walked Kerry to her door (no mention of coming in), said he'd "probably" see her at the party (strange since it was being held in the function room at The Swan, his parents' pub), given her a peck on the cheek (no attempt at a full-on kiss), and walked off, his head bowed. The sunny, carefree guy she'd first fallen for seemed to have disappeared altogether.

"Shall we go then?" said Sonja brightly, interrupting Kerry's gloomy recollections. "All set for a great time, Kez? I know I am!" She picked up her bag and opened the bedroom door.

Kerry followed glumly behind. She knew Sonja was being deliberately upbeat about the party. She was trying to cheer Kerry up after her awful evening with Ollie the night before.

At first, when Kerry had related what had happened, Sonja had told her off for not having the bottle to express her true feelings. But when she'd seen how upset Kerry was, Sonja had backed down, telling her not to worry and insisting that things would work out.

Kerry wasn't so sure.

When they walked through the doors of The Swan, the first person they bumped into was Ollie. To Kerry's mind, he looked as horrified to see her as she was him, and she immediately felt the tension between them. She groaned inwardly when Sonja made an excuse to go to the loo, no doubt to leave the unhappy couple together.

Kerry felt she had nothing more to say to Ollie; that the barrier between them was getting bigger and more impenetrable by the minute.

"Hi, Kerry, " he smiled. "You made it then?"

*Why wouldn't I?* Kerry felt like saying.

Instead, she replied, "Yeah and I'm dying to go the loo too. I'll see you later." Then she scurried off after Sonja, leaving Ollie looking slightly dazed.

Kerry spent the rest of the evening on tenterhooks. Her eyes constantly roved the room, looking out for Ollie, so that she could make sure she avoided him. When she did spot him, she turned her gaze away, but kept track of his whereabouts out of the corner of her eye.

At one point when she hadn't seen him for a while, she turned round from the bar with drinks for her and Sonja, and found herself staring right at him.

"I was just about to offer you a drink," he said, looking down at her. "I can get the next round in if you like."

"Thanks, Ollie," Kerry replied stiffly. "I'll let you know if we want one."

"Where are you sitting?" he continued.

"Uh, nowhere really, we're just wandering. Actually, I must get back to Sonja. She's being chatted up by a guy she's not interested in. I promised I'd rescue her after five minutes. See you later."

Kerry sidled past Ollie once more, relieved to

have escaped, yet feeling guilty about the dreadful way she was handling the situation. The trouble was, she didn't know how else to react.

Kerry wasn't the only person having a difficult time at the party. When Maya had arrived and spotted Billy chatting with Cat and Anna, she had felt the by now familiar pang of jealousy. It seemed that he was rapidly becoming an integral part of the gang and Maya still wasn't comfortable with the idea.

She watched from a distance as they stood by the stage, apparently engrossed in each other's conversation. There was a lot of laughter between them and they seemed oblivious to anything going on around them. If they *had* noticed Maya standing on her own a few metres away, then they weren't exactly falling over themselves to catch her attention.

*I might as well not be here*, she thought bitterly. *With Billy around, no one's interested in speaking to me.*

Maya thought about going home then reprimanded herself – this was, after all, one of the few times she was allowed out to a party like this. Her father had let her come because he knew and 'approved of' Robbie's parents.

Hell, why *should* she let Billy and her irrational feelings of jealousy spoil her evening? Maya put her Coke down on the nearest table and headed towards her friends.

As soon as she got near enough to overhear the conversation, she realised that Cat was in major flirt mode.

"Gosh, I never realised they were so big," she heard Cat squeal, her hand playfully squeezing the taut muscles on Billy's upper arm. "You must work out all the time."

"Not really," replied Billy, "but I like to keep fit. I play a lot of sport, mostly football."

"Wow. Your thigh muscles must be in even better shape then," Cat tittered. "I bet you could give Michael Owen a run for his money."

Billy shot a beseeching glance at Anna, who was standing grinning beside Cat. Anybody could see he was mortified to be the subject of Cat's unwanted attention.

He was wondering how he could shake her off without hurting her feelings (although, from the little he'd experienced of her, he wasn't entirely sure Cat had any feelings) when he spotted Maya.

"Hi, Maya," Billy called, anxious to divert attention. "How's it going?"

"Great," Maya replied, unable to contain a snigger. "You guys look like you're having a good time."

"Billy was just about to show off his six-pack, weren't you, Billy?" said Cat, running a fuchsiataloned hand down the front of Billy's canary yellow shirt.

"Actually, I was just about to get a drink," he replied, desperate to escape Cat's clutches. "What would you girls like?"

"Hey, why don't I come with you?" Cat twittered, spidery eyes fluttering unashamedly. The look of horror on Billy's face struck a chord with both Anna and Maya. They shot each other a conspiratorial glance, then Maya spoke.

"Actually, Cat, I only came over to say how great you looked. Is that a new hair colour?"

Cat preened visibly. If there was one thing that could distract her from a boy, then this was it. Turning her back on a grateful-looking Billy, who immediately scarpered, her face lit up like a light bulb at the compliment.

"Thanks, Maya," she beamed, smoothing her hand over her shocking violet locks. "Actually, it's one I made up myself at college. It was supposed to come out more of a mahogany colour, but I think I prefer it like this."

"Yeah, it goes well with the nails. Are they false?" asked Anna.

"Totally," Cat purred. "I put them on after I got ready tonight. The only trouble is, they're so long I'm scared to go to the loo in case I lose one in my knickers."

She broke off to listen to the track Matt – who was on DJ-duty – had just put on. "Hey, this one's great – shall we dance?"

The three of them waded into the thick of throbbing bodies and danced for a while, Cat giving it loads as usual, as if she was on *Top of the Pops*. Then Maya spotted Ollie on his own by one of the vast speakers. He had a bottle of beer in his hand and seemed to be staring into the distance, unaware of the frenetic noise and movement all round him.

*He looks like he needs some company*, she thought.

"I'll just go and grab Ollie," she yelled to the others above the music, and backed off the dance floor towards him.

"Hi, Ollie!" she called in his ear. Ollie turned towards her, a blank expression on his face. Seeing who it was, he then gave her a broad smile, lifted the bottle and took a glug of beer.

"All right, Maya?"

"Great. How about you?"

"I'm fine."

"Where's Kerry? Is she here?"

"Yeah, she's around. We haven't had much of a chance to speak to each other yet."

He felt like adding, *probably because she's been avoiding me all night*. But there was no point burdening Maya with his problems and he didn't think now was the right time to be having a heart-to-heart with one of Kerry's closest friends.

After making the effort to speak to Kerry and being met with all the warmth of an ice block, Ollie had given up. He was still feeling wretched about the way things had turned out the night before. If he'd stuck to his guns and insisted she told him what was up, as he'd been determined to do beforehand, they might be dancing together now. Instead, he was even less sure about the future of their relationship.

"D'you fancy a dance, Ollie?" Maya offered. "Cat and Anna are over there."

"Yeah, but let's not join the others," he replied. "I'm not feeling very sociable. Let's stay here."

"Sure," replied Maya, grabbing his hand and leading him to the very edge of the crowd of revellers.

For the next ten minutes or so, she and Ollie grooved to the rhythm of the music, saying nothing, lost in their own thoughts.

When Maya next turned to see if Anna and Cat were still dancing, she found they'd gone. She scoured the room, then saw Anna and Billy who, by now minus Cat, seemed to be having a very intimate conversation. Billy looked a whole lot more comfortable with Anna than he had done with Cat earlier.

Their faces were really close, almost touching, as they talked above the noise coming from Matt's DJ console. Each looked to be really interested in what the other was saying, nodding enthusiastically, arms waving to emphasise a point, eyes locked on to each other.

Maya turned away, her mind whizzing. She recalled a conversation she'd had with Cat and Sonja the day Billy had auditioned to join The Loud. Cat had told them that she was convinced Billy fancied Anna. Sonja and Maya had poopoohed the idea at the time, but perhaps, for once, Cat had been more perceptive than all of them...

# CHAPTER 8

● ● ● ● ● ● ● ● ● ● ● ● ● ● ● ● ● ● ● ● ● ● ● ● ●

## A RAY OF HOPE

Ollie skulked off to the family's living quarters upstairs from the pub just after ten o'clock, despondent and abandoning all pretence of being in a party mood. He had made several efforts to be with Kerry during the evening. Each time she had greeted him like nothing more than a vague acquaintance rather than her boyfriend of several months.

He noticed all too clearly how offhand she was, keen to get away, nervous even. In the end he'd given up and gone upstairs to watch the football on telly.

It was gone midnight when he came back down from his bedroom to check that the party had broken up and to see whether Matt needed a helping hand with all his gear.

When he walked into the room, there were just a few stragglers left behind and a couple of girls were helping his parents to clear up the plastic glasses, beer bottles and party popper innards that were strewn about the place.

He spotted Matt on the stage, expertly dismantling his DJ console. Ollie wandered up and jumped onstage next to him.

"All right, mate?" he asked. "Had a good night?"

"Yeah, no worries," replied Matt. "Especially once the aged relatives had gone off home. Then everyone really loosened up and got a bit livelier. It's been a good crack, even if I do say so myself."

"I saw Gabrielle was here earlier. Has she gone home?"

"Yeah, her older sister picked her up at eleven. She wasn't allowed to stay any longer."

"Are her parents quite strict then?"

"Something like that. It's funny, I don't think about her age at all until it comes to things like this. I mean, we can all do pretty much as we like, but my girlfriend has to be home by a certain time because she's only 14."

"Does it bug you?"

"Nah, not really. Anyway, she's worth it."

"Matt, you must really have it bad to be so understanding."

"I have." Matt stopped curling a power cable into a neat coil and shook his head slightly, grinning at the same time. "I don't know," he carried on. "I tell you, Ollie, I'm in love. Head over heels and all that slush."

"Yeah, I'd already heard," smiled Ollie. "Sonja told me earlier. I didn't quite believe it though – I wanted to hear it from the horse's mouth."

"Well, you just have. So now you know it's true. Scary, eh?"

"I'll say! I didn't think you were the type to fall in love."

"Neither did I. Especially not with someone so young."

"Should I start saving up for a new suit and a wedding present then?"

"Whoa, steady on!" laughed Matt. "I don't think we want to be going down that road just yet. One step at a time, eh?"

"But it must be serious! You've been going out for about a month now and you're not even two-timing her yet. At least, not as far as I'm aware..."

"That's right, I'm not. It is serious and before you ask, I don't plan on seducing her either. She's way too young."

"You plan on acting the perfect gentleman then?"

"Most definitely."

"What, even if she tries it on with you?"

Much as he wanted to believe Matt, even Ollie sounded a little sceptical now. But Matt was adamant.

"Yep," he said. "I'll just tell her I'm a virgin and hope she believes me."

"You're kidding! And you reckon you can carry on pretending you haven't had a string of girlfriends – like we all know you have – for the foreseeable future?"

"I'll do it for as long as it takes." Matt sounded determined. "I told you, I'm in love with Gabrielle and we've got a really special relationship. Anyway, I don't know why you're scoffing. Don't you think the same way about Kerry?"

Ollie gave a hoot of scornful laughter. "Jesus, man," he choked, "I don't know what I think about me and Kerry at the moment."

"How do you mean?" Matt asked, perplexed.

"Well, the way things are between me and Kerry, I reckon I'll be young, free and single again soon."

Matt looked totally surprised. "*Seriously?*" he said, not entirely sure if Ollie was joking. But one look at Ollie's face told him he wasn't. "I would have thought that if anyone had the perfect relationship then it was you and Kerry. What's gone wrong?"

Ollie grappled with the right words to say for a few moments. Then he tried to explain. "It's like she's pushing me away," he said. "All the time. I'm convinced she doesn't want to be with me any more. I think she's fed up with me..."

He broke off suddenly. He could feel his throat tighten as the awful reality of the situation suddenly hit home. He looked down at the floor to get himself back together before carrying on. "We hardly said a word to each other tonight. We might as well have been complete strangers. I felt as though she didn't want to be around me at all."

He looked up to see Matt shaking his head in dissent. "Y'know mate, it didn't look like that from where I was standing all evening. Whenever I spotted Kerry she was staring right at you. Usually from a distance, but she seemed keen to know what you were up to even if she wasn't with you."

"Really?" Ollie was taken by surprise. "I can't imagine why. Whenever I tried to catch her eye, she made sure she was looking in the opposite direction."

"Hmmm," said Matt frowning, as he tried to make sense of the situation. "So you haven't had a fight over anything specific?"

"Nope, not that I can see. But she's gone all cold on me, she's distant, doesn't want me to be around her at all. It's like she doesn't fancy me any more."

"I can't believe that, Ol. I'm convinced she thinks she's going out with Adam Rickitt," joked Matt. "You can tell by the way she looks at you. Are you sure it's nothing else?"

"Not unless it's so obscure I haven't sussed it out yet. God, she even shies away when I try and touch her..."

"What? Touch her *where*?" Matt grinned lustily.

"Shut up!" Ollie couldn't help but laugh at his friend's upfront attitude. "I mean like when I try and hold her hand or kiss her. She doesn't seem to want me near her."

"Well, maybe that's half the problem," Matt replied. "Maybe she's worried that you're getting *too* close. Maybe she's scared by what might happen..."

Ollie frowned as it dawned on him what Matt was getting at. "What, like she's worried one thing might lead to another...?"

"Exactly, Ol my boy. You're getting there."

"Oh."

"Have you actually done anything yet?" continued Matt.

"No."

"Because...?"

"Because, uh... I dunno really. I guess I don't want to force things. I figured we'd tackle it as and when we were ready."

"Well, I reckon you'd better start tackling it now. Because I'm willing to bet that's what the problem is."

Ollie looked away from Matt's triumphant face and scratched his head, trying to digest this new twist to the plot. "To be honest, I'd never given that a thought," he eventually replied. "But now you mention it..."

"It all adds up," Matt broke in. "Has to. I reckon if you think back to all the arguments you say you've been having, then look at it from Kerry's point of view and drop in the sex issue, you'll soon see the way her mind's working."

"D'you know, Matt? I think you might have something there. Or at least, I hope you have. If that's what's behind all this, then Kerry and I have got nothing to worry about."

For the first time in ages, Ollie felt a flicker of hope spark inside him.

## CHAPTER 9

●●●●●●●●●●●●●●●●●●●●●●●●●●●

### OLLIE TAKES CONTROL

Joe didn't go to the party at The Swan after all. He couldn't be bothered, even though it was only over the road. Instead, he stayed in his room, half-listening to the muffled bass thumping relentlessly from across the street.

He wasn't in the mood for partying, socialising, pretending to be cheerful. At the moment he couldn't bear to see Kerry and Ollie together, not when he felt so guilty for wanting them to be apart. *Permanently* apart.

He found it difficult to cope when his mind was in such a topsy-turvy state. He'd begun to wish more than anything else that he could stop loving Kerry. Then at least he could get on with his life, looking forward to the future rather than being stuck in limbo – waiting, hoping, wanting her to be his.

Joe picked up the little notepad from beside his bed and began flicking through it for the umpteenth time. It contained all his secrets, written in the form of songs, which he added to whenever he felt the need to express his feelings.

He'd spent most of the evening putting together the final touches to a love song he had been working on for months. It was for Kerry, though she would never know that. And it expressed all the love that he felt for her but could never, ever tell her.

Joe thought it was the best thing he had ever written.

• • •

Every time the café doorbell rang, Ollie looked up from whatever he was doing in the hope that it might be Kerry. He was desperate to see her, to talk to her, to make everything OK again between them.

After speaking to Matt last night he had decided to invite her round for something to eat at Nick's flat, one night in the week. It would give them both a chance to talk, to lay their cards on the table, in complete privacy.

In some ways he was glad Nick had asked him to work with Anna at the End today. It meant that he didn't have to make a big deal of calling Kerry up or going round to her house to ask her for this date. He wanted to keep things between them as light as possible, so that she wouldn't be on edge.

He had wondered whether Nick's was the best place for them to get together or whether, if she was worrying that he might pounce on her, she would feel intimidated about being there alone with him – assuming she agreed to come, of course.

But he had finally come to the conclusion that the advantages outweighed the disadvantages and that, because it was private, it was the best place for them to talk. Something they hadn't done properly for a while.

All he needed now was for her to come in the café.

The bell over the door rang again. Ollie stopped refilling the tray of ketchup bottles in front of him and looked up. It was Maya and Cat.

*Great,* he thought. Hopefully the rest of the gang wouldn't be far behind.

"Hi there, girls," Ollie called out cheerfully. "What can I get you?"

"A couple of Cokes please, Ol," said Cat, coming over to the counter and fishing some change out of her bag. "I didn't see much of you at the party last night. Where were you hiding?"

"To be honest, I was knackered, Cat," Ollie explained, taking a couple of glasses from the shelf behind him and two cans from the fridge. "And there was a really good match on the telly, so I wimped out and vegged instead. Did you have a good time?"

"Hmmm, it was OK." Cat pulled a less than enthusiastic face. "Unfortunately, there wasn't a single tasty guy there. The place was totally totty free."

"Poor Cat," sympathised Ollie, looking over at Maya and grinning broadly. "You must have been bored out of your mind."

"It wasn't *that* bad. Maya and I spent most of the night on the dance floor, didn't we, Maya?"

"Yeah," Maya laughed. "Until you were giving it so much one of your boobs nearly escaped from your dress, by which time I was so embarrassed, I had to leave you to it."

"It's not my fault Miss Selfridge don't make their dresses large enough up top for girls like me," huffed Cat. "It was a size 12 so it should have fitted."

Maya refrained from pointing out that while the rest of Cat might be a size 12, her boobs were at least a double D and therefore not likely to fit into anything like the same size. Instead, she raised her eyebrows at Ollie, took her Coke and headed for the window seat.

The door jangled again and Sonja and Kerry walked in, causing Ollie's heart to jump and his mind to go blank. As Kerry was behind Sonja, she didn't notice him for a moment; she headed straight for a seat next to Maya and immediately started to chat.

"Oh, hi, Ollie," Sonja announced. "Didn't see you there."

Kerry's head shot up and she looked over to the counter, surprised to see him.

They made eye contact and Ollie gave her a slightly shy grin which caused Kerry to feel even more awful about the way she'd behaved last night. Keen to make amends, though not entirely sure how, she stood up and went over to him.

"Hello, Kerry," said Ollie gently.

Kerry smiled hesitantly. "Hi. I didn't know you were working today."

"No, Nick asked me to do an extra shift. Apparently, there's a load of eight-year-olds coming in later for a birthday party. So it's all hands on deck. Anyway, how are you? What did you think of the party?"

Kerry wanted to blurt out that she'd had an awful time, that she felt dreadful about the way she'd been so off with Ollie, and how sorry she was.

But she didn't... couldn't... whatever. Instead,

she looked down at the vinyl floor tiles and muttered, "It was all right, I suppose..."

Ollie took a deep breath and launched into what he'd been wanting to say for days now. "Look, Kerry," he said quietly. "I have to talk to you. Not here, not now, but soon. There are things we need to sort out..."

Kerry looked up at Ollie, blinking rapidly. Tears were pricking the backs of her eyes and threatening to swamp her.

"Yes," she whispered. "I know. Me too."

"Will you come round to Nick's flat – on Tuesday, maybe? There's so much I need to say to you and I'd like to do it in private, if that's OK. What do you think?"

Kerry didn't hesitate. "Of course I will, Ollie."

# CHAPTER 10

● ● ● ● ● ● ● ● ● ● ● ● ● ● ● ● ● ● ● ● ● ● ● ● ● ● ● ● ● ●

## SUSSING OUT BILLY

"We want chips! We want chips! We want CHIPS!!"

Twelve impish faces followed Ollie and Anna as they hurried back and forth to the End kitchen laden down with plates, beakers of orange squash and cutlery. The hungry demands of a bunch of pre-pubescent boys and girls had reached such fever pitch that by the time their burgers and fish cakes and piles and piles of chips were ready, the noise inside the café was deafening.

"Remind me to say no next time Nick asks me to do a shift like this," Ollie chuckled to Anna as he bent down to mop up a spilt can of Coke from under one of their tables.

"Eurrrgh!" Ollie felt something warm and slimy dripping down the back of his neck. He reached up and scooped a baked bean encrusted soggy chip into his hand, then turned to see an impish-looking boy grinning at him.

"Joshua, that's really naughty," Ollie heard one of the mums bark. "Say sorry to the man at once."

"Sorry, Mr Man," the boy whispered, still grinning.

Ollie glanced over at Anna, who was trying desperately not to laugh, and wished it was home time.

"Oo-ee, Ollie, over here!" Ollie turned to the window seat where Sonja, Cat and Maya were still gossiping together. Cat was waving her empty glass at him.

"Could I have another Coke, *pleeeaaase*, Ol?" she whined in her best little girl voice.

"Coming right up, Cat," Ollie shouted cheerfully, though inside he was cursing her for not understanding how busy they were. It would have been much better if she had come up to the counter to get the drink herself. He also noticed that Kerry had left and wondered if that had anything to do with him.

*Stop being paranoid*, he scolded himself as he rushed back into the kitchen to pick up another order. *You've got nothing to worry about. Once Tuesday's out of the way, things'll be hunky-dory again.*

By the time he'd brought a can of Coke back to Cat, Matt and Gabrielle had joined the group.

"Hello, mate, you look hassled," Matt announced cheerfully.

"You're telling me," said Ollie, plonking the can on the table and heading back to the kitchen. "Can't stop. Let me know when you want something..."

"Sure, Ol. Me and Gabrielle are starving. We might run through the whole menu for you. Wouldn't want to see you slacking..."

"Cheers, mate," Ollie said in mock annoyance as he disappeared behind the coffee machine to make coffees for table four.

"Hello, Gabrielle," Cat purred, sensing an opportunity to wind Matt up. She knew he wouldn't be keen to let his girlfriend get too chummy with her. Cat knew way too much about Matt's numerous conquests and, having been one herself, she couldn't resist trying to make him sweat a little.

"Come and sit next to me," she ordered, patting the padded seat beside her. "We didn't get a chance to talk much last night. Did you leave early?"

"Yeah," Gabrielle replied. "I had to be home by eleven, or my dad would have killed me."

"Aw, poor Gaby," Cat pouted. "It must be difficult having a boyfriend so much older than you. Especially someone like Matt, what with him having a father who doesn't mind what he gets up to..."

"Oh, Matt's really understanding," said Gabrielle sweetly. "He always makes sure he gets me home at the time I'm told. He says he doesn't mind and that he's not that big a party animal anyway."

"Gosh, really?" Cat said, noticing that Matt was squirming a little in his seat. "That's interesting. I always remember Matt burning the candle at both..."

"Gabrielle, have you looked at the menu yet?" Matt cut in, desperately trying to kick Cat's leg under the table. "Only I'm starving. What are you going to have?"

Gabrielle obligingly looked away to study the menu, while Matt gave Cat ferocious looks across the table.

"Hey, Matt, guess who I saw in the Plaza yesterday?" Cat carried on blithely. "Josie Wilson. You remember her, don't you, Matt?"

Matt could hardly forget Josie. Looking back on it, he realised he'd treated her very badly, only taking her out when it suited him or if he'd had nothing better to do. And when she'd tackled him about it, he told her she was dumped, in front of all her friends.

Matt's face turned white, while he grappled around in his head for an appropriate response. He would kill Cat later. He *knew* it was a bad idea bringing Gabrielle to the café, but she'd wanted to meet up with his friends again. If her told her she couldn't, she'd only get suspicious.

Fortunately, Sonja took pity on him.

"Oh, yeah, I remember her," she answered Cat. "She was the one who was desperate to go out with you, wasn't she, Matt? Hassled you for months and couldn't accept that you weren't interested. The other guys thought you were a complete dork because she was so gorgeous."

"Yeah, that's the one," Matt agreed, grinning, while Cat pulled a face and took a slurp of Coke. She could see that she would be up against it here, so decided to back down – for the time being at least.

Just then the bell above the door jangled once more. When Maya saw who the newcomer was her face went blank.

"Hi, Maya," said Billy, coming right up to her and her friends. "I just popped in to see if Joe or Ollie were around."

"Hello, Billy," Maya said. "Ollie's in the back and I'm off to the loo." She stood up and headed towards the back of the café.

Although Billy had been to Maiden Bay with

them, this was the first time he had "just popped in" to the café on his own. Maya could imagine him sitting with her friends all afternoon, getting all involved and pally and irritatingly cosy with everyone. Because she still had to come to terms with Billy becoming a regular member of the crowd, she felt it was a worrying development.

In fact, when she came back from the toilet, Maya saw that Billy was standing by the serving counter talking to Anna. She remembered the way they'd been last night. She studied their body language now as she walked slowly back to the others.

And she realised that what Cat had sussed out long before the rest of them, really was the case. Billy fancied Anna.

She thought back to last night. Then, Billy was being really full-on with his body language and, while Anna wasn't backing off exactly, she wasn't giving him the come-on either. She obviously hadn't clocked what he was up to any more than Sonja or Maya had!

I wonder how long it'll be before Anna realises what's going on. And I wonder what her reaction will be. Somehow Maya couldn't see the mature, deep-thinking Anna going for someone as unsophisticated as Billy.

Although she'd not seen it at first, now Maya

understood what was going on with Billy, she felt a lot more comfortable about having him on the scene. Now it made sense why he'd been so full-on recently. OK, so he wanted to get chummy with the gang, but he obviously had an ulterior motive. Hanging out with the others was a way of getting to see Anna and sound out her feelings for him.

Somehow, Billy fancying Anna made things different. Maya had, after all, decided on their trip to Maiden Bay that she didn't fancy Billy herself.

When she thought about it hard, she knew the crowd meant a great deal to her. She was very possessive of the friendships that she'd formed. Maya now realised that what had also been worrying her was that somebody new might just upset the delicate chemistry that made it all work so well. And Maya would hate to see anything go wrong. She needed her friends.

She understood at last that she'd been uncomfortable with Billy hanging around because she would blame herself if things went wrong, as she had inadvertently introduced him to the group.

However, it was reassuring to Maya that Anna had been drawn into the group, and that seemed to be working out OK. And if Anna and Billy got together, then maybe things would, in some way, even out. So perhaps it was time to accept Billy into the circle.

But Maya wasn't sure that it was fair to leave Anna in the dark.

*I think I should tell her what Billy's up to*, she decided.

# CHAPTER 11

● ● ● ● ● ● ● ● ● ● ● ● ● ● ● ● ● ● ● ● ● ● ● ● ● ● ●

## GOING FOR A SONG

Kerry felt as nervous as if it was a first date. This meeting up with Ollie to talk through their problems – and then doing anything *but* – had been going on for long enough.

It was getting quite ridiculous, Kerry realised. She was beginning to feel desperate and had given herself the deadline of tonight to finally confront Ollie with her fears.

But she felt uneasy about the fact that they were meeting in Nick's flat. When Ollie had invited her in the café on Sunday morning, she had been feeling so guilty about the party the night before, she would have agreed to meet him anywhere, if it would make things better between them.

Now she wasn't so sure.

"Hello, Ollie," she managed to squeak as she stood on Nick's doorstep.

"Kerry, hi, come on up."

Kerry gingerly climbed the stairs to Nick's flat above the record shop. She found it unnerving enough that she'd never been in here before; the fact that Ollie was staying here alone made her feel even more edgy.

As he led her into the sitting room, Kerry had half expected to find that the flat had the same musty feel as the shop below, so was pleasantly surprised to find herself in a large, airy room painted in a tasteful shade of blue and with a lovely, deep-pile cream carpet on the floor.

The living space above the record shop was a lot bigger than that of Anna's tiny flat next door. It almost had the feel of a luxury apartment, Kerry thought. Nick had obviously taken the best flat for himself and rented out the smaller one to make a bit of extra cash.

A black leather-look sofa and chairs and glass-topped coffee table gave clues as to the era Nick felt most comfortable with. And the game was completely given away by the numerous photos on the walls of him in his roadie days posing with scary-looking glam rock bands from the '70s.

"He hasn't changed one bit, has he?" Ollie commented as he watched Kerry study one picture after another. "His hair is as long now, if not longer, and I swear I saw him wearing that same T-shirt only last week. Only the beer belly's changed size," he added, chuckling.

Kerry wandered into the kitchen/dining room and was taken aback by the display Ollie had presented on the table. It was laid out like an upmarket restaurant, with napkins and shiny cutlery, wine glasses and a basket of French bread. In the middle of the table was a tiny cut-glass vase containing a single red rose.

Kerry blushed when she saw it. Ollie had obviously gone to a huge effort to make it look as romantic as possible.

"Ollie, this is lovely," she said, which of course it was. She didn't add that it made her feel as if she was about to play a part in the great seduction scene of a low-budget movie. Or that it made her want to run out of there, back to the safety of her own home.

"I wanted this evening to be special," Ollie explained, a little embarrassed. Then, trying to lighten the mood, he added, "I hope I don't poison you with the food."

Kerry gave him a shy smile and wandered over to the pan of food on the cooker. It was a brownish-red mass of *something*, bubbling away merrily alongside a huge pan of spaghetti.

"Bolognaise," said Ollie.

"It looks great. How many people are you expecting?"

Ollie laughed easily. "I know. I'm not too good at judging quantities," he explained. "I bet I'll still be eating it when Nick gets back. Anyway, Madam, if you'd like to sit down, dinner is ready to be served."

Ollie held out a chair for Kerry. He took the napkin off her plate and folded it over his arm like a top waiter, then, when she'd sat down, placed it with great flourish across her lap. He was trying his best to be funny and over the top, but Kerry began to feel more and more flustered.

"Thank you," she said quietly. "I'm sure I don't deserve all this trouble."

"Yes, you do," Ollie said. He was tempted to launch into the big speech he had half planned in his head, the one where he would tell her just how special she was, and how much he loved and cared for her. But he stopped himself.

*There will be time for that later in the evening,* he thought. *Let's just try and have a nice, argument-free meal first.*

Keen to keep her on his side, Ollie spent much of their meal recalling the first few months of their romance, reminding Kerry of the funny little incidents that had bonded them in those early days.

The approach seemed to work; he could feel Kerry relaxing into her seat, playing along with the game. Then, just as he was about to launch into the way he felt about her, the doorbell rang.

Reluctantly, Ollie got up and went downstairs to answer it. He couldn't imagine who would be calling on him at this time of night. He would have ignored it, but Kerry urged him to go, saying it might be something important.

The sight of Joe on the doorstep surprised him.

"Hi, Ollie," Joe said. "How's it going?"

"Joe, hi, what are you doing here?"

Joe could sense the tension in Ollie's voice. He immediately felt he was unwelcome. "I... uh, came round to see how you were getting on... and to bring you these."

His outstretched hand held several sheets of A4 paper. Ollie took them and glanced over the words imprinted on each sheet.

"Some new songs," said Joe simply. "I thought we could go over them, maybe put together some music. But... if now is a bad time..."

"That's great, Joe," Ollie tried to sound as enthusiastic as he could. He knew how fragile Joe's confidence could be – one negative word and it would shatter into a thousand tiny shards. And he remembered the conversation he'd had with Kerry last week. If Joe was feeling low, he didn't need Ollie adding to his problems by being anything less than positive.

Ollie chose his words carefully. "I can't wait to look at them. But the truth is, mate, Kerry's here, we're having a meal and trying to iron out a few glitches. You know?"

"I'm sorry, Ol!" Joe was mortified. He only wished Ollie had warned him – he would never have deliberately interrupted. "I had no idea. I wouldn't have dreamt of coming round if I'd known."

"It's OK," Ollie smiled. "Don't worry. Look, can I keep hold of these? I'll look at them later, then maybe we could get together tomorrow night?"

Joe was already backing away, nodding vigorously. "Of course, Ol, whatever you say. I'll catch up with you tomorrow." Then he turned round and disappeared into the night, completely embarrassed.

Ollie went back up to the sitting room and absent-mindedly put the songs on the coffee table. Then he hurried back to Kerry who was still sitting at the table, toying with her dessert.

"Sorry about that," he said. "It was Joe, just calling round for a chat."

"Oh. Why didn't you invite him in?" asked

Kerry. She would have welcomed the sight of anyone at the moment; as far as Kerry was concerned, this was turning into an excruciatingly embarrassing evening.

"I... er, got the feeling he didn't want to interrupt," Ollie replied, a little perplexed.

*Interrupt what exactly?* an angry voice in Kerry's head yelled. But she managed not to say anything negative, putting down her spoon and forcing a strained smile.

"Oh, well, never mind. I expect you'll see him soon enough," she said, desperately trying not to lose her cool. "That was a lovely meal, Ollie. Thank you."

"That's OK. Look, why don't you go and sit in the living room? I'll get some coffee on."

Kerry wandered back into the other room and deliberately chose to sit in one of the armchairs, rather than the two-seater settee. She looked at the pile of music magazines on the coffee table, then noticed the papers that Ollie had just dropped there.

Curious, Kerry picked them up and began reading the top sheet. From the format, Kerry guessed it was a song, no doubt one Ollie had been working on for The Loud. It was called *Distant Lovers*.

She read on...

*I know that you're so far away*
*I know you're out of reach*
*You wonder how I hear your voice*
*When we hardly even speak*

*Distant lovers all the same*
*Distant lovers it's not a game*

Kerry's eyes flickered over the rest of the song, her eyebrows knitted together and her forehead creased in deep concentration.

She studied the words over and over again. This was a song written by Ollie about someone he cared for deeply.

And it wasn't her.

Her mind raced ahead, interpreting the meaning of the words.

Then it hit her: the song must be about Elaine, Ollie's ex-girlfriend. They had split up when Elaine had decided to go travelling the world earlier in the year.

But it was obvious from this that she was still on Ollie's mind. All the stuff about being far away and out of reach, it was a definite reference to the many thousands of miles between them. And then, later in the song, there were lines about how the distance didn't matter, how he knew they'd be together one day.

*Oh, my God...* thought Kerry. *He's still in love with her!*

Kerry was so engrossed in the words, she didn't notice Ollie come back into the room carrying two mugs of coffee.

As soon as he saw what she was reading, Ollie realised he should have been more careful about where he'd left Joe's songs. Joe would be mortified if Kerry found out he wrote the stuff for The Loud.

Sensing Ollie was in the room, Kerry looked up and caught his gaze. He had guilt written all over his face.

"What are these, Ollie?" she asked flatly, though she already knew the answer.

"They're, um... some songs Joe and I have been working on," Ollie replied as evasively as possible.

"Joe? You and Joe?" Kerry had never heard Ollie mention that Joe had anything to do with the songwriting side of things before.

"What's Joe's input into them?" she asked. Her voice was cool and calm, and belied the anger that was welling up inside her.

"Well, he kind of says what he thinks of the words and we, erm, try to get the music down together," Ollie replied, still vague. "That's what we were talking about earlier."

"But you actually write the songs?"

"Er, I guess so..."

Kerry stood up trembling. She could hardly believe this was happening to her.

*How could I have got it so wrong?* she thought.

Kerry suddenly felt very naive indeed. Stupidly, she had been thinking Ollie was in love with her, when all the while he was still wrapped up in Elaine.

Even more hurtful was the fact that he was trying to get Kerry into bed, while at the same time being in love with someone else.

*This can't get any worse*, thought Kerry. *I can't believe he's been lying to me all this time.*

"Kez, what's wrong?" Ollie put the coffees on the table and gently reached out to put his arms around Kerry.

"Get away from me, Ollie," Kerry hissed, pushing him roughly away. "I don't want you near me."

"Kerry! What is it? What's wrong? Have I done something?"

Kerry was so angry she could hardly speak. "Why didn't you tell me?" she said, her voice shaking with emotion.

"Tell you what?"

"Th– th– that..."

Kerry broke off, unable to put into words what she was trying to say.

Instead, she stormed past Ollie. He watched in despair as she grabbed her coat and clattered down the stairs, flung open the front door and ran off down the street, sobbing loudly.

# CHAPTER 12

●●●●●●●●●●●●●●●●●●●●●●●●●●●●●

## KERRY CALLS IT OFF

"Oh– oh... Sonja, I feel so... so... s-s-stupid. I d-d-don't know what to do."

Kerry stood in the Harveys' hallway, tears streaming down her face, her nose rubbed red and her eyes puffy and mascara-smudged. She wasn't entirely sure why she had come here straight after leaving Ollie's, but she knew she couldn't go home looking like this.

Sonja put her arm around Kerry's shoulder and gently led her upstairs to her room. "Come on," she said gently. "Don't worry, it's OK."

Kerry was surprised to see Maya sitting on Sonja's bed, surrounded by textbooks.

"Oh, Maya," Kerry sobbed. "I'm s-so glad you're here too."

"Kerry! What on earth's wrong?" Maya leapt

up from the bed and threw her arms around her friend.

"It's Ollie," Kerry replied, sniffing. "We're f-f-finished." As she heard herself say those final words, Kerry broke down once more and began sobbing uncontrollably.

Sonja reached for a handful of tissues and passed them to her friend, easing her down on to the bed.

"It's OK, Kez," she soothed. "Take your time. Start from the beginning and don't forget to breathe."

As instructed, Kerry took in huge breaths of air between sobs and gradually began to calm down again. She buried her face in the pile of tissues and tried speaking again.

"I went to Ollie's for dinner, like we'd arranged," she said. "And it was really awful – the whole evening just felt wrong."

"What do you mean?" Maya asked. "Why did it feel wrong?"

"Oh, I don't know. I felt under pressure the whole time I was there. He was making a real effort to be nice, but it felt weird me being completely on my own with him in Nick's flat."

"Why, Kerry?" probed Sonja. "I thought he'd wanted to talk to you; you didn't think he was going to pounce on you, did you?"

"No, it wasn't that. But it put me on edge.

Although we were having a nice meal, making small talk, it was like we were skirting round the real reason we were there. I just wanted to get it over and done with."

"So why didn't you?" Sonja had a note of irritation in her voice. She couldn't understand Kerry pussyfooting around like this; *she* would have had it out long since.

"Because I was too scared, too much of a wimp. Stupid, I know, but that was the reason. So anyway, after we'd finished eating, I went into the sitting room while he made coffee and I saw some songs that he'd written. I picked them up and started reading them. And.. and... and the first one I saw was a love song..."

Remembering some of the lines that she'd read, Kerry broke off again and started weeping.

"And?" Sonja encouraged. "What happened then?"

"Well, it was obvious! Ollie had written this song about Elaine."

As Kerry stopped to blow her nose, Sonja and Maya exchanged glances as if to say, "So?"

"OK," Maya said. "So the love song was about Elaine. Does that really matter, Kerry? After all, they did go out for quite a while before Ollie and you got together. And you knew that he cared for her, didn't you?"

"Yes, b-b-but you don't understand. It was about n-*now*, today. It was saying how much he *still* loved her, how he was *in* love with her. It wasn't about the past..."

"Oh." Sonja nodded sagely, as if she now knew where Kerry was coming from. "What did Ollie have to say about all this?"

"He didn't," Kerry went on. "I didn't give him the chance. Or, at least, I tried to, but the words wouldn't come out. I was so upset, I ran out."

"Oh." Maya stroked Kerry's mass of curls and glanced at Sonja again. She could see from the look on her face that Sonja was thinking exactly the same as Maya was: *Kerry, are you sure about this?*

Sometimes, Kerry's inability to communicate with Ollie amazed Maya. She couldn't understand how Kerry could explain her feelings to her girlfriends perfectly adequately, yet not be able to say what she meant to Ollie.

*Maybe it's something to do with boy-girl relationships*, Maya thought. Maybe the same thing would happen to her when she fell in love.

"But Kerry," said Sonja gently, "are you absolutely positive the song was about Elaine and not you?"

"Oh, yes, believe me, I'm sure," Kerry said definitely. "There was stuff in there that couldn't possibly relate to me. Truly. And it was so beautifully written, it was obvious he meant every word."

"And you're sure it was Ollie who wrote the song?"

"Yes, he told me he did."

"Could it not just be something Ollie made up, you know, because it happened to rhyme or something? It's not as though you found a letter to Elaine, is it? Surely a song can be as much of a fantasy as anything." Maya was trying to break it to Kerry gently that she might have got hold of the wrong end of the stick – again.

"No, Maya, it wasn't like that," said Kerry adamantly. "You should have seen the look on his face when he realised I'd read the songs. He's guilty. Ollie still loves Elaine, I'm sure of that. So as far as I'm concerned, we're finished. I never want to see him again."

• • •

It was just after 8.00 am when the phone rang in the Harvey household and Sonja's mum shouted up the stairs that it was for her. Dragging herself from under her snug duvet, Sonja picked up her extension and grumbled a muffled "Hello?" into the receiver.

She heard Maya's crisp, wide-awake tones on the other end of the line. "Sorry for calling so early, Son, but I wanted to speak to you about Kerry," she said. "It was impossible to talk last night when she was around and I wasn't sure I'd get the chance at college today. I wanted to know what you thought about everything she said."

Sonja said nothing for a moment, gathering her thoughts together about the previous evening.

One of the reasons she had overslept was because she'd spent several hours in bed after Kerry and Maya had left, mulling over what had been said. She had come to some definite conclusions on the subject.

"Well, now that you're asking," she said, "I think Kerry's got it totally wrong."

"Yeah, so do I."

"I think she's using the song thing as just another excuse not to confront the real issue."

"Which is still sex," said Maya matter-of-factly.

"Exactly. She's become so hung up about it that she'll do anything not to discuss it with Ollie. Even if it means ending the relationship."

"Which would be crazy. I've never met two people who were so right for each other."

"Me neither."

Sonja thought for a moment. "Do you think

one of us ought to have a word with Ollie? Y'know, put him in the picture?"

"Absolutely not! We can't interfere that much. Kerry would never forgive us. No, we need to be more subtle than that. We've got to somehow *force* them to talk to each other. Even if we have to shut them in a cupboard and tell them they're staying there until they sort it out."

"Hmmm. Actually, Maya, you've just given me an idea..."

# CHAPTER 13

• • • • • • • • • • • • • • • • • • • • • • • • • •

## JOE GETS A SHOCK

It was with some trepidation that Joe called on Ollie at Nick's flat early on Wednesday evening. He would have much preferred to stay while Ollie read through his songs last night. That way he could have gauged Ollie's initial reaction to them.

Although Ollie always took Joe's songs seriously, treating them with great respect, there was a hugely insecure part of Joe's psyche that half expected his friend to burst out laughing after he'd read them and say how useless they were.

He was particularly worried about what Ollie would think of *Distant Lovers*. It was a song so dear to Joe's heart, he would be devastated if Ollie thought it was rubbish.

Although he had read and re-read it a thousand times, and thought it was pretty good, he was terrified that his judgement was clouded by his emotions.

Ollie had done little other than study the same song ever since last night. He'd been trying to work out what it was about the evening, and more particularly the song, that had set Kerry off. As far as she was concerned, Ollie had written it, but what was in there to upset her so much? It was only a song after all.

Ollie was pleased when Joe knocked on the door. He was keen to grill Joe about the lyrics.

"You know that song *Distant Lovers*?" he asked, as he made coffee in Nick's kitchen.

"Yes?" said Joe, shuffling his feet nervously, dreading what might come next.

"Well, did you write it with anyone in mind?"

Joe felt the blood drain from his face. "Wh-wh-what do you mean?" he stuttered, deathly white.

"It's just that Kerry happened to see it..."

Joe took a gulp of hot coffee and began spluttering uncontrollably, as much through fear of what was coming next as the scalding sensation that seared his throat.

"Hey, I'm sorry, mate," continued Ollie, "I didn't mean her to see it. She just picked the whole lot of songs right up off the table and started reading. But I never let on that you'd written them, you don't need to worry about that. I told her they were mine."

"S-so what happened?"

"Well, she flipped. Burst into tears. Ran out of the flat. Like she was really mad at me."

"Why?" Joe said, suddenly intrigued.

"Dunno, mate. She never said. Something really upset her and though I've looked and looked at that song, I can't for the life of me see what it was that sent her overboard like that. That's why I wondered if it'd been written for anyone specifically. Like maybe I was missing something?"

"No, it wasn't, Ol," lied Joe. "I made the whole thing up."

"That's what I thought. So why d'you think she ran out like that?"

Joe was stumped. "Er, hormones?" he finally suggested, lamely.

"I tell you, she tried to blame it on her hormones the last time we met. If it is, it's the longest bout of PMS I've ever come across. She's been like this for weeks," said Ollie ruefully.

"So you didn't get to iron out the glitches then?"

"Far from it," Ollie sighed. "Nothing was sorted – it went from bad to worse."

Ollie fleetingly wondered whether to mention the conversation he'd had with Matt on Saturday night. Then he decided against it. Anything to do with the subject of sex was bound to embarrass Joe. Ollie figured Joe had so little experience with girls that there wasn't a lot that he could contribute to resolve the problem, if it really was sex, other than a few uncomfortable silences and much shuffling of feet.

"D'you know what? I think I'm just about ready to give up on Kerry," he continued, desperately. "I can't work her out any more, she's become a complete stranger to me."

Joe looked down at the floor, unsure of what to say.

"I thought we'd have it all sorted out by now," Ollie carried on. "But the way things are going, it might as well be over between us."

"I'm sorry, Ollie," Joe managed in a small voice. "I really hope you're wrong."

"So do I, mate," Ollie said. "So do I."

Suddenly aware that Joe was probably sick of him going on and on about Kerry, Ollie changed the subject. "Anyway, you didn't come here to listen to me moan on, did you? Let's change the record."

Joe smiled shyly. "It's OK, I don't mind, honestly. But if you really do want to talk about something else, you could start by telling me what you thought of my songs."

"Oh, Joe, I'm *sorry*. I didn't think. They're brilliant. Your best yet. And *Distant Lovers* is the most gorgeous song I've ever heard. I've already thought of some music for it. Actually," he said, suddenly animated, "I forgot to tell you. Billy called into the café on Sunday. Do you remember a while back when he spoke about a bass player he knew – some guy called Andy?"

"Yeah, I remember. He's on the photography course with Billy and Maya, isn't he?" Joe recalled Billy mentioning Andy while everyone was at the beach one day at the end of the summer holidays. He'd assumed the guy wasn't interested in auditioning for The Loud as Billy hadn't mentioned him since.

"That's right," Ollie carried on. "Well, apparently he hasn't been on the course for a few weeks, but Billy bumped into him last week and he's really keen to meet up with us. Isn't that great?"

Joe was made up. "Brilliant," he smiled. "When do we get to meet him?"

"The only time he can make it over the next few days is Saturday morning, when I'm supposed to be working. But if you guys can make it then too, I'll square it with Anna and Dot to see if I can get half an hour off. What do you think?"

"Sure," Joe grinned. "Count me in. Hey, won't it be great if this works out?"

Ollie knew Joe would be pleased. It might help cheer him up a bit. It certainly raised his own self-esteem a few notches.

"The Loud, resurrected and back to its full glory," enthused Ollie. "At least that'll be something to look forward to in my life."

# CHAPTER 14

● ● ● ● ● ● ● ● ● ● ● ● ● ● ● ● ● ● ● ● ● ● ● ● ● ● ●

## GETTING IT TOGETHER

Maya spent most of her lunchbreak on Thursday trying to track down Joe. She had hoped to catch him on his way out of double English, but by the time she'd raced over from her science class on the other side of St Mark's campus, he'd already gone.

After trawling the cafeteria, sixth-form study room, library and music block, she finally discovered him sitting on a wall overlooking the park opposite the school. He was staring into the distance, swinging his legs, lost in thought.

"Hello, Joe, I've been looking everywhere for you." Maya pulled herself up on the wall next to him and smiled warmly. She hadn't seen much of him recently, and she was a little shocked to see how tired and drawn he looked.

"Have you?" he replied, surprised. "Why, what's up?"

"We-ll," Maya decided to cut the small talk and launch into the purpose of her mission. "Have you heard about the rows Kerry and Ollie have been having?"

"Yeah," Joe nodded. "I saw Ollie last night. He's pretty cut up about what's been going on."

"So is Kerry. But she won't talk to him."

"Oh."

Maya wanted Joe to give her more than just an "oh". He was Ollie's closest friend, after all. She was hoping he would be able to shed some light on Ollie's point of view in all this. She waited a while, hoping that there was more to come from Joe.

There was.

"Ollie told me he was ready to give up on her," Joe finally explained. "He's pretty fed up with the whole situation."

"I thought as much," said Maya. "Look, Joe, we've got to get them to talk *properly*. Will you help?"

"Sure, why wouldn't I?" Joe turned to look at Maya, his face crumpled into a frown.

"Oh, I don't know..." Maya shrugged, buying time in order to choose her words carefully. Although Joe had refused to admit his feelings for

Kerry out loud, Maya was sure her intuition was right. Joe was in love with Kerry. Something told her as much every time she looked at him.

"I know you're pretty involved in it all," she carried on, "what with Ollie being your best friend. And I know you're pretty close to Kerry, too..."

"You mean you still think I'm in love with her?" Joe blushed and nervously scuffed the heels of his boots on the wall behind him.

Maya looked away, embarrassed. She didn't want to hassle him any more, not if he was going to keep on denying it. "Joe, I'm sorry about that," she said hurriedly. "I must have got the wrong idea that day on the beach."

"Actually, you didn't..."

She stared at him open-mouthed. "So it *is* true?"

"Yes." Joe looked down at the ground. There, he'd said it, once and for all. He wasn't sure why he'd suddenly admitted it after all this time – he certainly hadn't intended to. It just popped out. Perhaps he just couldn't hold it all in any longer.

"Oh, Joe, I don't know what to say..."

"There isn't much *to* say. Kerry has no idea, nor does Ollie. Nor anyone else, except you. And I'd like it to stay that way..." his voice trailed off.

"Of course. But how do you feel about it? Especially with everything that's been going on between them recently?"

Joe studied his feet. He felt uncomfortable discussing his feelings, especially as he'd kept these ones a secret for so long. He wasn't sure what to say or how to say it.

"It feels weird," he said simply.

"I'm sorry," Maya sympathised. "You must feel stuck in the middle of it all."

"It's OK, I want to help. Honestly. I'll do anything I can to keep them together."

As he spoke, Joe realised how much he meant what he was saying. In spite of everything that had been going through his head recently, he didn't really want Ollie and Kerry to break up. And he had an idea that offering to do his bit to keep them together might help him to get rid of some of the guilt he'd been feeling.

"Are you sure, Joe?" probed Maya.

"I'm sure. But please, Maya, *please* don't tell anyone else about me and Kerry. You won't, will you?"

"Of course not."

"OK. What do you want me to do?"

• • •

"So I take it you won't want to be hanging out at the café for the next few years then?"

Sonja and Kerry had just walked past the End

and were heading home after their last class of the day. Normally, they might pitch into the café for a drink and somewhere to hang out for a while. But not today. Kerry was adamant she must go home.

"Oh, I'm sorry, Son," wailed Kerry. "I feel terrible about the way this has worked out. I don't want to go to the café in case Ollie is there, but at the same time I hate having to avoid the place. The last thing I want to do is stop hanging out with everyone, but the fact that the main place we do get together is the End makes it really difficult for me."

"I know," Sonja soothed. "It's OK, I understand."

"Before I started going out with Ollie we all fitted into the gang like one big happy family. It's always worried me that we could spoil things if it all went wrong between us. But then, at the same time, I guess I never thought we'd actually split up..."

Sonja stopped herself from pointing out that they hadn't actually split up yet, or that she and her friends weren't going to let them. Instead, she nodded sympathetically, indulging Kerry in her current state of mind.

"Well, if you don't fancy hanging out with everyone, why don't we go out tomorrow night? Just the two of us."

"I dunno," Kerry sighed. "I'm not sure that I'm that much fun to go out with at the moment."

"Well then, I'm just the person to cheer you up. Come on, we could go for a burger, maybe see what's on at the pictures, hang out at one of the cafés in the Plaza. It's got to be better than sitting in on your own all evening, feeling sorry for yourself. Hasn't it?"

Sonja could be very persuasive when she wanted and Kerry found herself nodding before she'd had time to think of an excuse.

• • •

Maya was on her second mission of the day. She was taking a quick detour in the rain to Anna's flat before going off to the train station to meet her sister Sunny from an out-of-town school geography trip.

She had a book Anna had lent her – *Understanding Your Inner Psyche* – and she had promised to take it back. It was also a good excuse to have a quick chat to Anna about Billy.

Anna hustled her into her flat from the drizzle outside and insisted she stay for a drink.

"I'm glad you called round, Maya," she said. "I wanted to ask a favour."

"Oh, yes? What is it?"

"Well, it's about your birthday on Sunday."

"*Ye-es...*"

"You said you were all meeting for a meal, but you didn't say what time. Only I'll be working that day and I really want to come, but I won't get off from the café until just after three..."

"That's fine," Maya cut in. "We won't eat until after four; just come along when you're ready."

"Oh, Maya thanks, that's great."

"I'm glad you'll be able to make it," Maya said. "I know it must be difficult what with the strange hours you work."

"Yeah, it can be a bit anti-social at times. But no matter, it keeps me occupied. Can I get you a drink?"

"I'd love an orange juice, please," Maya replied, "but I mustn't be long or I'll be late for Sunny's train. She's been on a field trip to study rock formations on the coast today; her train will be here in ten minutes."

Anna filled two glasses with orange juice and motioned for Maya to sit down.

"Did you enjoy the party on Saturday night?"

"It was OK," Maya replied ambivalently. "Actually..." She broke off, now wondering whether she should say anything or not. Then she decided it was only fair to tell Anna what she suspected. "I wanted to ask you something about Billy."

"Go on then, fire away."

"It was just that you two seemed to be getting on really well at the party. I wondered whether you liked him."

"Oh, yeah," Anna enthused. "He seems like a really nice guy."

"No, what I mean is, do you *fancy* him?"

Anna's eyes opened so they were the size of saucers and she looked incredulously at Maya. "Oh, God, no!" she said, half laughing, half horrified. "Whatever gave you that idea?"

"Well, nothing really," Maya replied, almost chuckling to herself. Anna looked completely gobsmacked.

"What I mean," Maya went on, "is that I didn't think you fancied him. But I'm pretty sure Billy fancies you."

Oh," said Anna flatly, "I see. What makes you think that?"

"Just the way he is with you. He's being pretty obvious. Even Cat's noticed. In fact, she was the one who sussed it first. Sonja and I thought she was making it up. But it's true, Anna. He's always asking about you, at photography class, or whenever you're not around.

Anna turned away for a moment and stared out of the window. Then she spoke.

"To be honest, Maya, I've never given it a

thought. Getting involved with someone has been way down on my agenda for months now. And I certainly hadn't contemplated anything happening with Billy. Like I say, he's a nice guy, but not in *that* department." She turned back to Maya and smiled. "So you don't have to worry about me cramping your style..."

"Oh, no!" Maya gasped. Anna had got completely the wrong end of the stick. "*I'm* not after him. Not at all. Billy and I are just good friends. No, it's just that I thought I ought to put you in the picture, so you know where you stand. I kind of sussed that you weren't aware he was making a play for you. I thought I was the most naive girl in Winstead when it comes to guys, but you've been coming a pretty close second recently."

Anna burst out laughing. "You're right. I think I'm not bad at working out what's going on between other people, but when it comes to myself, I'm useless!"

She picked up the book that Maya had laid down on the table. "I read all this stuff about psychoanalysis and I still miss the obvious."

"Mmm, you don't normally miss much when it comes to the rest of us, do you?" said Maya a little ruefully. "Anyway, I'm glad I told you. Look, I'd better go now or I'll be late."

"Yeah, sure, Maya. And thanks for coming round. I appreciate it."

After Maya had gone Anna sat down with a glass of wine and pondered what had just been said. When she thought about it, there *were* a couple of incidents with Billy where she should have worked out that he fancied her.

Now, as she contemplated the possible consequences of what Maya had said, she knew immediately she wasn't ready to start seeing anyone yet. Her ex, David, had been very bad news and Anna knew that she was nowhere near ready to give her trust to anyone. Not even to cute, harmless Billy.

David had been responsible for so much – the unwanted pregnancy and the consequent split with her mother. When she thought about it, it was hardly surprising that Anna hadn't noticed the amount of attention Billy had been paying to her. She had a lot on her mind at the moment, what with her mother coming down to see her on Saturday.

It would be the first contact they'd had in over a year and it was a meeting Anna was absolutely dreading.

## CHAPTER 15

● ● ● ● ● ● ● ● ● ● ● ● ● ● ● ● ● ● ● ● ● ● ● ●

### FANCY MEETING YOU HERE...

Ollie stood outside Burger King in the high street and looked at his watch. It was 6.55 pm. He was a little early.

Walking through the door, his eyes combed the busy restaurant looking for Joe. Once he was sure his friend wasn't already inside, Ollie walked back out again, propped himself up against one of the vast floor-to-ceiling windows near the door... and waited.

He had been puzzling over the phone conversation he'd had with Joe last night, and still had no idea why his friend wanted to see him so urgently.

Joe had insisted he couldn't wait until Saturday morning when they were meeting up anyway, and he wouldn't be drawn into telling Ollie over the phone. Nor would he pop over from his house opposite – which, to Ollie, would have been the most obvious thing to do.

No, all that Joe kept saying was, "It's really important that I see you, Ol; promise me you'll be there."

Ollie leaned against the window and rhythmically tapped the back of his head against the glass. He'd had an overwhelming feeling of numbness throughout his body ever since that awful scene with Kerry on Tuesday evening, and he found the dull thud of his skull on the glass strangely comforting. At least he knew his body was still alive and functioning, even if his emotions had switched off.

Ollie hadn't seen or heard from Kerry since that night and knew she was avoiding him. Likewise, he hadn't made any effort to contact her.

He couldn't see the point at the moment. It wasn't as though he could *force* her to tell him what was going on in her head. He didn't want to put any more pressure on her and had decided it was best to wait for her to make the first move.

Not that he was entirely sure she would.

By twenty past seven, Ollie was beginning to get fed up. And he was starving. The smell of burgers wafting up his nostrils every time someone opened the door was playing havoc with his stomach juices.

Perhaps he could stave off the hunger a bit if he moved away from the door, he thought.

Ollie straightened himself up from the slouch he'd adopted against the glass and decided to take a walk along the High Street. He wasn't aware of the person coming along the road towards him until it was too late.

"Oouff!" he said as he cannoned into the hurrying figure.

"Kerry!"

"Ollie!"

They each took a step backwards and registered the shock on the other's face.

Ollie was the first to gather his thoughts well enough to speak. "Um, I'm sorry, Kerry," he said tentatively, "I didn't see you there."

"Hello, Ollie," came the guarded reply. "It's OK, I wasn't looking where I was going. And I was rushing. I'm supposed to be meeting Sonja outside Burger King and I'm really late."

"Well, she's not here yet," said Ollie. "I've been there since five to seven myself, waiting for Joe, and neither of them have turned up."

"Oh." Kerry turned away and stared through the window.

*Damn!* she thought. *What a rotten time to bump into Ollie.* She couldn't think of anything else to say.

"It's odd that Joe hasn't showed up," Ollie continued. "He's not usually late for anything." He gave a little ironic laugh.

Then his brain began ticking over and he began to wonder if he and Kerry were being set up. It was a bit suspicious that they had both been told to meet at the *same* place at the *same* time on the *same* evening. *And* that their respective dates weren't here.

Ollie looked at Kerry and watched as her head turned towards him and he saw that she wore the same expression on her face as he imagined was on his. It was a look that said, *They haven't, have they?*

"Do you think Sonja and Joe planned this?" asked Kerry, frowning.

"Urr, I wouldn't put it past them," Ollie said. "It does seem a bit suspicious."

"What the heck did they think they were doing?" she demanded, her nostrils flaring.

"Maybe they thought it was the only way to get us talking," said Ollie simply.

"Yeah, you're probably right," Kerry agreed. "I bet it was Sonja's idea."

"Well, it's kind of working so far," said Ollie hopefully. Then, before Kerry could say any more, he added, "Look, do you fancy getting something to eat, now that we're both here? I don't know about you but I'm famished."

Kerry stared at the scuff marks on her shoes for what seemed like an eternity before replying. "Uh, no, Ollie. I don't think I will, thanks. I think I'll just go home."

"Kerry, if you walk away from me now, we might as well forget it. We'll be finished. Is that what you really want?"

Kerry could hear the note of desperation in Ollie's voice, but the issuing of an ultimatum only stirred up her anger once more.

"OK, Ollie," she said stiffly, "if you really want to know the answer to that, then yes, it is what I want. There isn't any point us carrying on anyway. Not when you're in love with someone else."

With that, she turned round and set off purposefully down the road, back towards home.

Ollie chased after her. "What?" he said incredulously as he caught up with her up and walked alongside. "What on *earth* are you talking about?"

"Elaine, Ollie, as if you need it spelling out. How can you go out with me when you're still in love with her?"

"*What?*" repeated Ollie. "*Elaine?* I'm *not* in love with her. Whatever gave you that idea?"

"That song you wrote, *Distant Lovers*. It was

all about being in love with someone far away... which is what she is. And... and the way you described how you felt about her. It certainly wasn't about me, Ollie. So it has to be about her."

Kerry was standing facing him in the street now. Her face was flushed and her chin quivering as she tried to control her emotions.

"Kerry, you've got to believe me, that song wasn't about Elaine. It was completely made up." Ollie thought frantically for a way to make her believe him.

"I promise you, Kerry," he finally said, "on my mother's life."

Kerry's eyes studied every inch of his face. She could see immediately that he was telling the truth.

Yet instead of instant relief, Kerry felt herself getting even more upset. Her throat tightened till she couldn't breathe and a tidal wave of tears began coursing uncontrollably down her face. She felt completely wretched.

"Oh, Ollie," she wailed, lowering her head into her hands to cover her shame. "I feel like such a fool. I'm so confused, I think my head is going to explode."

Ollie took her gently by the arm and guided her to a wooden bench by the side of the road. He sat down beside her and looked out at the constant stream of slow-moving vehicles crawling along to the junction with the High Street.

"Kerry, you've got to tell me what all this is really about," he begged. "I know it's not about Elaine and that song. *This* has been going on for weeks."

"But it's going to sound so stupid..." Kerry wailed, her head still in her hands.

Ollie turned and rested his fingers lightly on her shoulders. Slowly, she let her hands drop to her lap and looked at him shyly through her unruly mop of hair. Ollie decided to get his thoughts out into the open once and for all.

"Kerry, you know I love you more than anything in the world," he said earnestly. "You mean everything to me, and I hate seeing you unhappy like this. So – and you can tell me if I'm way off the mark here – has all this got something to do with sex?"

Embarrassed, Kerry looked quickly away and began staring at the pavement. "Kind of," she said in a small voice.

"Well, what is it? Come on," he urged. "Please talk to me. What are you worried about?"

"I-I guess I don't want to s-s-spoil things between us," she said, her voice quivering. "Although I think I've done a pretty good job of that already these last few weeks."

She broke off and peeped shyly at him out of the corner of her eye. His face oozed sympathy. She gave him an uncertain smile before carrying on.

"It probably doesn't mean so much to you, but for me it's a really big thing. I've never slept with anyone before and I'm so worried in case it changes things between us. I guess all I want is for everything to stay the same."

Ollie looked a little perplexed. "But what's made you so anxious about it? What have I done? I haven't been putting any pressure on you to sleep with me, have I?"

"Well, no, I– I guess not," Kerry muttered. "I think I've been putting pressure on myself, if I'm honest. I suppose I keep thinking that the longer we go out together, the closer we're going to come to sleeping together. And that thought scares me. I just don't want us to change, Ol. Or at least, not yet, anyway."

"You know, it needn't be any different between us," said Ollie gently. "Not if we don't let it. And you're wrong about it not meaning much to me. It's as important to me as it is to you. I just worry now that you think I want us to take things further, before you're ready…"

"No, it's not that, Ol. But I keep thinking that you must want us to sleep together at some point, and don't get me wrong, I do too. But I'm *scared*."

Once again her chin began quivering and two big droplets of tears plopped over her long eyelashes and trickled down her face. Ollie lifted one hand and wiped them away.

"It's OK, Kez," he said, "I understand. I care for you more than you'll ever know and I want it to be right between us. And if that means waiting for a month, or a year, or as long as it takes, then so be it. It's no big deal, not really."

He lifted a hand and brushed away a little tear that had begun sliding its way down her cheek.

"Sleeping together is only a small part of what we have, Kez," he said. "The most important thing is that we love each other and look out for each other. Nothing else matters as much. Don't you agree?"

"Oh, Ollie," Kerry sobbed, the tears in free-fall down her face now. "I've been such an idiot. I've built this whole thing up into so much more than I should have. And you've stuck by me even though I've been a total mess. I don't deserve you."

Ollie put his arms gently round Kerry's shuddering body and lightly kissed the top of her head. In return, he felt her arms wrap around him and they sat hugging each other, saying nothing.

"So does that mean we're OK again?" Ollie asked finally.

Kerry lifted her head and looked at him with such love and tenderness in her eyes that he already knew the answer to the question.

## CHAPTER 16

● ● ● ● ● ● ● ● ● ● ● ● ● ● ● ● ● ● ● ● ● ● ● ● ● ● ● ●

### A NEW BEGINNING

Anna flicked a duster over the TV and began sorting through a pile of books heaped on the living room floor. She'd been up since 6.00 am, not because she particularly wanted the flat to look nice for her mother's arrival, but because she couldn't sleep.

She'd been blocking out the feeling of dread she'd had in the pit of her stomach ever since she'd agreed to the visit nearly two weeks ago. Every time she'd thought about it, she'd pushed aside her anxiety, calming her nerves with the promise that she'd worry about it when the time came.

Now the time *had* come. And Anna was fighting the wave of sickness that was threatening to overwhelm her. Her mouth was dry and her head pounded as she moved briskly around the flat, cleaning and tidying, all the while fretting about how the afternoon was going to pan out.

Owen had rung yesterday to say that their train was due in at 11.02 am. At 11.15 when the doorbell went Anna knew they had arrived. There was no backing out now.

Taking a deep breath to calm herself, Anna took one last look at the flat, checked her face in the mirror in the kitchen and opened the door.

Owen stood at the top of the steps clasping a bunch of flowers, a big smile on his face.

"Hello, Anna," he said as cheerily as always. "It's so good to see you again!"

Throwing his arms round her neck, he gave her a big bear-hug. It helped ease some of the tension in Anna's body, though only temporarily. Over Owen's shoulder she could see her mother coming up the steps behind him.

Anna drew away and gave her brother a nervous look, moving aside to let him into the flat. Then she looked towards her mother who was by now standing on the top step, slightly out of breath and watching her daughter's every move.

"Hello, Mum, how are you?" Anna asked politely.

"Much better for seeing you," replied Mrs

Michaels tearfully. "It's been such a long time."

Anna sensed that her mum was about to hug her too; instinctively she felt she wasn't comfortable with that, so she stepped back into the flat to let her come through the door.

"Here, let me take your coat," Anna said, watching while Mrs Michaels undid the buttons on the ancient brown woollen coat Anna remembered from when she was a child.

She couldn't help but notice how much older her mum looked. Hair that had been greying was now white in parts. The lines on her face had become trenches. She had lost weight, her skin was sallow – she looked more like her grandmother than her mother. Anna suddenly felt sorry for her.

Mrs Michaels gazed around the kitchen and sitting room area. "It looks like a nice place you've got here," she said. "You've made it really homely."

"Yes, I like it," Anna agreed. "I'm very happy here."

"That's nice, love."

Anna felt a little uneasy with this sudden familiarity. The last time they had spoken Mrs Michaels had called her all the names under the sun; now she was "love" again as though nothing had happened.

"Come and sit down and I'll make us a cup of tea," she said, trying to dismiss the prickly tension she was beginning to feel under her skin.

"I think I need to pop to the bathroom first," said Mrs Michaels, so Owen showed her where it was before following Anna into the kitchen area.

"She's acting as though nothing's happened," Anna hissed as she noisily clattered tea things on to work surfaces.

"Well, what do you expect her to do, Anna? Come in here and confront the problem without even saying hello? She's incredibly nervous about this and she's dealing with it in the only way she knows how."

"OK, OK. I guess I just want to get it over and done with, I mean, she's not the only one who's nervous."

"I know, but give her a chance. At least let her have a cup of tea before you air your grievances."

"All right, Owen. You probably know how to handle her better than I do."

The Michaels family spent the next hour talking about everything other than the reason they were together. A host of trivial subjects was dissected, from the workings of the café and how much business Nick turned over, to the regularity and appalling filthiness of trains to Winstead, to the high cost of housing in the south of England compared to the north.

Anna politely asked after all her mother's

friends and was regaled with stories of what they and all Anna's old schoolmates were getting up to now. By this time Mrs Michaels had relaxed, her mouth was on a roll and she let slip that one of Anna's friends had given birth to a little boy, "totally out of the blue, never said a word to anyone".

Then she rattled on about how the girl was living in a council flat and how beautiful the baby was and suddenly she looked up and saw the pain etched on the face of her only daughter.

"Oh, Anna, I'm so sorry," she said, her voice tight with emotion as she tried not to cry. "Me and my big mouth," she whispered before bursting into tears.

Anna sat transfixed by the sight of her sobbing mother. She'd never seen her fall apart like this before and it was a bizarre contrast to the rage she'd witnessed the last time they'd talked. Anna suddenly felt stronger than she had done at any time in the last year.

"I never meant for you to leave," Mrs Michaels wept. "It's something I've regretted ever since. But I was so angry. I thought you were such a sensible girl, much brighter than all your friends. I never thought it would be my daughter who got into trouble, never. And when you told me you were going to– to... get rid of the baby... well, it broke my heart."

She took a tissue from her bag and wiped her eyes and streaming nose. "There hasn't been one day since when I haven't regretted what happened. I should have stood by you. It was your life and your decision. I should have been there for you and supported you."

She looked at Anna through pools of tears, a wretched shell of a woman riddled with guilt and sorrow. Anna's heart went out to her.

"It's all right," Anna said, her own eyes filling with tears. "I was angry with you for a long time, for all those reasons you've mentioned. I really needed you, Mum. I was so scared when I found out I was pregnant, I didn't know what to do. I was stuck in a relationship that had gone wrong and I needed someone to help me get through it. And you weren't there for me. That was what made me so mad."

"I know, love. And I'll never forgive myself for the way I acted. But it was such a shock, a terrible shock."

"I realise that; it was to me too. But then to have you telling me it was going to ruin your life as well as mine... well, that was just about the final kick in the teeth for me. I couldn't believe you'd be so... selfish."

"You're right," Mrs Michaels sighed. "I didn't think before I spoke, that's always been my biggest problem. I shouldn't have been worrying about myself, about what the neighbours and the Church would think, it was the least of our worries. I'm so sorry, I don't know what else to say."

"I know, Mum. And look," said Anna, softening, "maybe neither of us handled it very well. Perhaps I shouldn't have told you at all. But you see – for a little while at least – a tiny part of me wanted to keep the baby. I knew I wouldn't get any support from David, but I thought if I told you, you'd help me get through it."

Anna paused and looked at her mother before continuing. "I guess I didn't expect you to be so dead against it. And yet, at the same time, you didn't want me to go through with the abortion. I was so lost. What was I supposed to do? You didn't want me to keep the baby, but you didn't want me to have a termination either. Oh, Mum, you just didn't seem to care." Anna knew this would hurt, but she had to say it.

Mrs Michaels' body shook as she wept openly at the memory of what had happened.

"I should have been on your side," she wailed. "If I had, perhaps you wouldn't have done what you had to do. It's all my fault."

"No, Mum, you're wrong if you think I would have kept the baby," said Anna firmly. "In the end, I would have had the abortion anyway. You know, it wasn't a decision I took lightly, but it was the right thing for me to do at that time."

Sighing, Anna sipped at her now tepid tea. "I just wish I hadn't told you about it the way I did. I think I deliberately threw the abortion in your face to make you even more angry, and for that I'm sorry."

Anna went over to where her mother was sitting and knelt down in front of her. She took her by the hand and gave it a squeeze. "We've both said and done some terrible things," she said gently. "But perhaps we can begin to put all this behind us now? If we can forgive each other, maybe we can start again? What do you say?"

"Oh, I'd like that very much," Mrs Michaels replied. Leaning forward in her seat she bent down and gave Anna a hug for the first time in over a year.

Anna prayed that perhaps now their conflict was finally coming to an end.

## CHAPTER 17

●●●●●●●●●●●●●●●●●●●●●●●●●●●

### THINGS CAN ONLY GET BETTER

"I'm so pleased you two are finally getting things sorted out," Maya enthused to Kerry in the café on Saturday lunchtime.

"Yeah and if I'm not mistaken it's all thanks to you and Sonja," smiled Kerry. Leaning over the table she gave first Maya, then Sonja, who was sitting next to her, a grateful hug.

"Well, if we'd left it to you two, you still wouldn't be talking," Sonja laughed. "I bet you were horrified when you walked up to Burger King and saw Ollie there instead of me."

"I was pretty much! But it didn't take us long to realise we'd been set up and who by."

"Someone had to do something, Kez."

"I know. And it made me realise how lucky I am to have friends like you guys. So, er, thanks."

"Aw, shucks," Sonja said in a show of mock bashfulness. "Really, it was nothing. At least you're back on track together at last. Where is Ollie, by the way?"

"He should be here now," said Kerry, looking at her watch. "He was meeting up with Joe and Billy and another guy to see about getting The Loud together again this morning. But he promised Dorothy he'd only be gone half an hour. He was due back ten minutes ago. I don't know where he's got to."

"Of *course*," Maya nodded, "the penny's just dropped. Anna's not in today, is she, because she's got her mum and Owen coming down to visit? I wondered why you were tarted up like that, Son."

"Cheek!" Sonja laughed, recognising the irony in Maya's words.

Sonja was the person *least* likely to get "tarted up". She didn't need to, with her perfect skin and model-like features and figure. Her beauty was totally natural.

Even so, she had spent an extra ten minutes getting ready this morning, in the hope that she might bump into Owen.

"I would like to see him again," she swooned. "Even though I know there's no mileage in it, with him living so far away. But the occasional sighting and perhaps a snog would at least help to keep my spirits up."

"I don't suppose you've found out yet whether he's staying the weekend?" Kerry ventured.

"No, Anna had no idea. I thought I'd call up to the flat later on. See if I can catch him in."

Kerry was distracted by someone tapping on the window outside the café. Turning to look, her face broke into a grin as she realised it was Ollie. Grinning back, he pulled a funny face then came up to his side of the window and planted a kiss on it.

Kerry blushed, smiled shyly and gave him a little wave.

"Eurch," Sonja groaned. "You know, that's the worst thing about couples getting back together. They always have to go all soppy on you, like they're star-struck lovers all over again."

Kerry didn't care that Sonja was taking the mick. Her eyes followed Ollie as he came bounding into the café and kissed her on the lips.

"Hi, guys!" he called. "Got to dash. Poor Dot'll be having kittens if I don't get my backside in the kitchen right now."

"How did the band meeting go?" asked Kerry as Ollie dashed towards the staff side of the End.

"Brilliant!" he shouted, disappearing round the corner into the back. "Couldn't have been better.

The rest of the guys are on their way. They'll tell you all about it."

Just then Joe, Billy and another guy, closely followed by Cat, came hurrying inside.

Sonja couldn't resist ribbing the boys. "We hear you lot are ready for your stadium tour," she chuckled, "and that you're about to give the Manics a run for their money."

Joe laughed a little nervously and felt his face colour.

"I hope you're not going to go all pop-starry and refuse to sit with us," Sonja continued, winking at Maya and Kerry.

"We were just going to choose some music from the juke box, then we'll be right over," said Billy. "Er... I don't suppose anyone's seen Anna?"

"It's her day off," Maya replied. "She might pop in later if you're lucky."

"Hope so," said Billy wistfully. Realising he might have let on more than he wanted to, Billy's face flushed a little and he lifted his hand to his short dark hair and gave his head a scratch. "I... er, wanted to talk to her about something," he explained to Maya.

The boys sloped off to the Nick's juke box while Cat slid into the seat next to Kerry.

"I've just followed that guy's bottom in here," she said in a loud voice, indicating Andy's rear end. "God, it's cute. Really pert. Does anyone know who it belongs to?"

"His name's Andy," Kerry explained. "He's the new fourth member of The Loud."

"Ooh, goody! So I might be seeing a lot more of him then – if you know what I mean..." Cat let out a high-pitched squeal at her little joke and continued to stare at the backside of Andy, who was blissfully unaware that she had chosen him to be her next victim.

"Hey, did I tell you lot my good news?" she carried on, suddenly beaming. She looked round at the girls' faces and was met with blank stares from all three.

"Obviously not. Well, I've been asked to do the make-up for the college's end-of-year theatre production. Isn't that great?"

"Fabulous," said Maya. "What are they putting on?"

"Cinderella. Apparently, of all the people on the beauty therapy course, I was their first choice. I couldn't believe it!"

"It was probably because they knew you'd have no trouble doing the Ugly Sisters," cackled Sonja. "After all, you do your own face every day."

"Ooh, we are being bitchy today, aren't we?" Cat poked her tongue out at her cousin and returned to drooling over Andy's back view.

When the boys trooped back en masse, Cat made a great show of sliding along the seat and patting the empty spot next to her.

"Come and sit next to me, Andy," she cooed. "It's nice to have someone new to talk to for a change."

Unaware of what he was letting himself in for, Andy said a grateful "Thanks" and slipped into the seat alongside her.

It gave everyone the chance to study the new lad. He was tallish and slight with black, spiky hair and pale skin. An open face and crinkly eyes made him look friendly and approachable, and he did have the kind of cute, boy-band looks girls swoon over.

He also looked as though he wouldn't last five minutes in the company of chew 'em up and spit 'em out Cat.

"OK, boys, what are you having? My treat..." Ollie was back at the table, his notebook open and ready to take orders. He had a huge smile on his face and seemed totally relaxed and happy with his lot.

Maya hadn't seen him look as content as this in weeks. Kerry was the same: at ease, comfortable, buoyant. It made the interfering she and Sonja had done worthwhile.

The boys noisily shouted out their orders while

Ollie scribbled away, occasionally glancing at Kerry tenderly, as if he couldn't bear to take his eyes off her. In turn, she kept looking at him adoringly, not daring to let him out of her sight too long in case he went away again.

No one noticed the exchanges more than Joe. And he was pleased for them, even though it made his heart ache.

It was good to see his friends happy again. He knew it wasn't the best possible outcome for him, but realistically, what chance did he have with Kerry anyway, whether Ollie was in the picture or not?

Joe was glad he'd done his bit to bring them back together. It vindicated him of the guilt he'd been dragging around inside him for such a long time.

And anyway, now he had something else to focus on.

The meeting with Andy that morning had gone better than Joe could ever have hoped. They'd all got on well; it felt like they were all coming from the same direction and everything seemed to gel.

It turned out that Andy also enjoyed writing songs and was keen to be involved in the creative side of things too. But he genuinely seemed to love the songs that Joe had written, and Joe didn't mind a bit that it was Ollie getting all the praise instead of him.

Now all they had to do was keep plugging away, get some rehearsals under their belts and arrange some gigs.

It would be an uphill task, but Joe was revelling in the challenge.

# CHAPTER 18

● ● ● ● ● ● ● ● ● ● ● ● ● ● ● ● ● ● ● ● ● ● ● ● ● ●

## PARTY ANIMALS

"OK, guys, it's twenty past four. You lot will get me shot if you don't all leave now."

Ollie stood in the middle of the café waving his arms around and trying to get everyone's attention above the din. Unfortunately, no one seemed to be paying any attention to what he was saying.

The table by the window resembled a children's tea party with empty cans and glasses, napkins and spilt food and drink strewn all over the place. The noisy chatter, as people tried to make themselves heard above everyone else, was earsplitting. It was hard to believe only nine people were left in the place, not ninety.

There was an impromptu party going on. OK, so it wasn't the most sophisticated do in the world – no dance floor, no fancy lighting and the music blaring from the juke box was prehistoric. But with the gang by now out in force, they were making up for the lack of facilities with as much noise, mess and banter as possible.

Like all the best parties it had been completely spontaneous. Matt and Gabrielle had wandered into the café soon after Cat, and since then no one seemed keen to leave or to have anything better to do on a Saturday afternoon.

Only Kerry appeared to be paying any attention to the SOS calls Ollie had been making for the last twenty minutes.

"Come on, guys, we'd better go," she'd suggested, first to Sonja, then Maya, then to anyone who happened to be within earshot. No one took any notice.

Eventually, Anna came into the café to see what was going on. She wore a look of amused disbelief on her face.

"Crikey, Ol, what's happening?" she asked. "It sounds like there's a riot going on from upstairs."

"Anna, I'm sorry, they're not getting on your nerves, are they?" Ollie's voice was earnest, even though he had a wry grin on his face. "It just sort of happened and now no one seems to want to leave."

Anna's eyes sparkled – she liked to see

everyone having a good time. "No, it's cool," she said. "Owen's just seeing Mum off at the station, so we might even join in when he gets back."

Sonja, who by some miracle had overheard the conversation, piped up. "So does that mean he's definitely coming back?"

"Yes, Sonja," Anna said. "You'll be pleased to hear he's staying overnight and going back in the morning."

"The party's carrying on at yours then, is it, Anna?" said Sonja cheekily.

Anna faltered before answering. She wasn't sure she'd feel comfortable having that many people in her tiny flat. Nor would she feel happy about having Billy there, not after what Maya had told her.

Fortunately, Ollie came to her rescue.

"Or we could all go to Nick's," he suggested. "He said I could have people round so long as I left the place as I found it. He's pretty cool about stuff like that."

Matt, who on hearing the word party had immediately pricked up his ears, added, "Yeah, great idea, Ol. Let's all go and trash Nick's place."

"So that's sorted," Ollie grinned. "Everyone back to Nick's place – except for Matt who'd better bugger off home."

● ● ●

"So, Andy, would you like to see my tattoo?"

Cat leaned against the wall in Nick's kitchen, one elbow cupping her head, her free hand twirling a pigtail expertly dyed in Ravishing Brunette. Andy was virtually pinned against the wall, an amused expression on his face.

"Sure, Cat," he said, "so long as it isn't anywhere boring."

"Ooh, no, you don't have to worry about that. It's on one of my erogenous zones. Look..."

She undid the bottom three buttons of her baby blue cardie and wiggled her bare stomach at him suggestively.

Sonja walked in to get a drink from the fridge and wasn't at all surprised to see that Cat was up to her usual antics.

"Hang on," she said, peering a little closer at the Cupid on Cat's tummy. Then she added triumphantly, "I *knew* it was fake."

"Wh-what do you mean?" stuttered Cat.

"Last week when you were displaying your wares to all and sundry, that tattoo was above your belly button," Sonja pointed out. "*Now* it's underneath."

Cat shook her head. "No, Son, you've got it wrong. It's always been there. How could I possibly move it? That doesn't make sense."

"It's just a transfer, Cat," said Sonja,

exasperated. "You could put it on top of your head if you wanted. I don't know why you keep insisting it's real. Any fool can see that it's not."

Sonja flounced out of the room, leaving Cat to carry on with her seduction as best she could.

"She's just jealous," Cat explained to Andy. "She'd love a tattoo, but she faints at the sight of blood. And she's no good with needles. You can touch it if you want."

Cat stuck out her stomach a little further and gave Andy no option other than to put out his hand and poke the tattoo. Cat squealed with excitement.

"You've got really cold hands," she giggled. "I know a good way to warm them up for you, if you like." She fluttered her eyelashes and took a sip from her glass.

*This is going well*, she thought. *I reckon I'll have him in the bag by the end of the evening – no problem.*

Andy smirked and took another swig of ice-cold cider from the bottle he was holding. His dark eyes glinted as mischievously as her own.

"Sounds interesting," he drawled, holding out his free hand and letting it rest lightly on the bare skin of her waist. "I'm ready when you are..."

"Ooh, no, not here," Cat giggled, "not when someone might walk in on us..."

"Later then, Cat," he replied, grinning wickedly. "When we've got to know each other a bit better..."

"Mmm," purred Cat, inching her way a step closer to him, "sounds good to me."

Back in the living room, Ollie had pushed all the furniture to the walls to reveal a makeshift, shag-pile dance floor. Matt had nipped home to get some of his best compilation tapes and was now in charge of Nick's ancient stereo.

"I can't believe he hasn't even got a CD player," he complained to Gabrielle. "I've never met anyone old enough not to have one before. It's like not having a telephone."

"You could have brought some of your stuff back, couldn't you?"

"Are you kidding, Gab? It cost £6000 and sits on a reinforced floor. It would be ruined in seconds in a place like this. Anyway, someone might knock into it or scratch it or something."

Gabrielle smiled. She liked the fact that Matt was so protective of his music equipment – it was cute. She thought everything about Matt Ryan was cute. He was also funny, kind, gentle, gorgeous... she could go on for days.

Matt turned up Nick's stereo so that his favourite thrash track could blare out. Immediately, the window panes began reverberating against the heavy bass, threatening to jump out of their wooden frames.

Ollie dimmed the lights and took centre stage with Matt and Andy. Soon they were whirling round and round, arms and legs flailing like a bunch of maniacs.

Joe and Billy watched from the sidelines with Cat, Kerry, Gabrielle and Maya.

"Mmm, he's so cute," Cat drooled to no one in particular, "and look at the way he moves. He's all hips and bum. Irresistible!"

"I take it you're on about Andy," said Kerry.

"So you really fancy your chances with him then, Cat?" Maya asked.

"It's a foregone conclusion," smirked Cat. "He's already begging for a snog. I can tell."

Billy, who stood on the periphery of the conversation, felt he had to butt in.

"Er, Cat?"

"Yeah?" she said vaguely, swaying her hips and concentrating on Andy's every move.

"You didn't know then? Andy's gay."

● ● ●

"Where did Sonja and Owen get to?"

Ollie and Kerry were sprawled on the settee together, their bodies entwined, completely danced out. It was late and the party had finally broken up, leaving them to ponder the evening's events.

"I dunno," Ollie replied. "They disappeared hours ago. They were virtually glued to each other all night."

"I know. It's a shame Owen lives in Newcastle. They'd be really happy together, I'm sure."

"What, like we are?" asked Ollie.

"Yeah, just like we are."

Ollie gave Kerry's hand a little squeeze. "I'm so pleased we're back together again. I've really missed you."

"Mmm, me too." For a little while, they said nothing more, then Kerry turned slightly to face Ollie.

"Ollie," she ventured.

"Hmmmm?"

"Do you know what I'd really like?"

"What?"

"I'd really like it if we could just stay here like this and be close to each other. I've really missed being near to you these last few weeks..."

She broke off, momentarily taken aback by her own forthrightness. Kerry hadn't intended to say that, then all of a sudden it had popped into her brain and out of her mouth. Without her even thinking about it.

Quite unexpectedly, it felt comfortable putting her real feelings into words like that.

"Sure," Ollie replied. "But don't you have to get home? Your parents will be worried, won't they?"

"I told them I was staying at Sonja's tonight," said Kerry matter-of-factly.

"Kerry, *really*?"

"Oh, no, it wasn't a lie," Kerry retorted, reading his mind. "I was supposed to be staying there. We arranged it earlier – before this party even got off the ground. Before Sonja knew for certain that Owen was staying. Her parents are away for the weekend, so it's not as if they'll be wondering where I've got to."

"Oh, right. Well, that's great then, we can stay here like this for as long as you like. There's plenty of room for us both. Are you comfortable?"

"Mmmmmm." Kerry snuggled down a little further into Ollie's arms and closed her eyes. Within minutes they were both asleep.

## CHAPTER 19

● ● ● ● ● ● ● ● ● ● ● ● ● ● ● ● ● ● ● ● ● ● ● ● ● ●

### HAPPY ENDINGS

Kerry woke up to find light streaming through a chink in the curtains and Ollie's arms still wrapped around her.

*I could stay like this for ever*, she thought dreamily, *lying here, as close as any two people can be.*

She moved his right arm very slightly so that she could see his wristwatch. *Eight thirty. Mmmm, plenty of time yet.*

She snuggled into his body once more, revelling in the warmth of his skin... when an uncomfortable realisation hit her. She really needed the loo. *Damn.*

Kerry didn't want to wake Ollie so she gently moved his arms away from her body and slipped off the settee. Apart from a slightly muffled grunt or two, there was no other sound or movement from him.

She padded softly towards the bathroom at the far end of the hallway, dodging empty beer cans along the way. God, the place was a mess! They'd be here all day tidying up.

Kerry went to the loo, then stood over the washbasin, studying her face in the mirror. She immediately wished she hadn't. Her hair lay flat to her head on one side, no doubt from lying on Ollie's chest, and her eyes had turned into two small currants which peered back at her, blinking in horror. She sorely wished she'd taken her contact lenses out last night: they felt like pieces of grit in her eyes.

. Her skin had cultivated a nice layer of grease overnight, and what make-up she had worn the evening before – mascara and a little eye colour – had slid down her face so that she looked like something from a horror movie.

Kerry filled the basin with warm water and splashed her face in an attempt to bring it round. She ran her fingers through her hair to bounce it up a bit, then had another look at her reflection. There was a minor improvement, but not much, but enough.

She scoured the room looking for cosmetic help, though she didn't hold out much hope of finding anything in Nick's bathroom, not unless he was a secret transvestite.

Then she spotted it: a padded black make-up bag on the floor beside the loo. It looked familiar. It *was* familiar – it was Sonja's.

Kerry grabbed the bag which seemed to be stuffed more with receipts, bus passes and money than cosmetic goodies, and thanked whoever it was looking after her that morning.

She rifled through the bag and began the repair job. It wasn't as though Kerry wore very much make-up – like Sonja she didn't – but what little she did put on always gave her added confidence and was infinitely preferable to facing the world naked.

And she couldn't bear the thought of Ollie seeing her looking (as she thought) like the back end of a bus. Especially not after their first night spent together.

Kerry resolved in future to make sure she went out with more than the tiny bottle of perfume and Barely There lipstick in her bag. It would save a panic like this. Of course, she'd packed an overnight bag, but it was sitting uselessly at Sonja's where she'd left it yesterday morning.

As Kerry crept out of the bathroom once more she was startled to hear Nick's doorbell ring. Who on earth would be calling at this time on a Sunday morning?

She made her way downstairs and gingerly opened the door.

"Oh, Ol, sorry to bother..." Sonja looked up from the front page of the *Sunday Mirror* she'd been studying and stopped mid-sentence.

At the sight of Kerry standing at the door, her eyes grew to twice their size and her face broke into a knowing grin.

"Oh, *yeah*," she leered, "and what are *you* still doing here?"

Kerry blushed furiously. She knew how this must look and, however innocent she was, Sonja was going to take some convincing that nothing had gone on between her and Ollie.

"What have you been up to, you naughty little girl?" continued Sonja, her tone like that of a strict headmistress who'd just caught someone from Year Eight smoking in the toilets.

She raised her eyebrows skywards, a dreadful smirk on her face. "I take it you've been here all night. And I bet you didn't spend the night in Nick's bed – *alone* – did you?"

"We weren't in Nick's bed," Kerry answered, suddenly feeling very awkward.

"We being the Royal We, I presume," Sonja cut in. "As in 'my husband Ollie Stanton and I..'?"

"Something like that," blushed Kerry. "But we slept on the settee, if you must know. Fully clothed."

Sonja didn't believe Kerry for a minute. She'd have to make sure she took a look for herself while she was there.

"*Ohh*, of course," Sonja smirked again. "You know, I'm so pleased I came back for my make-up bag. Otherwise I bet you wouldn't have let on about this, would you, Kez?"

"Possibly not," Kerry admitted, a small smile breaking across her face. "Anyway, isn't it a bit early for you to be up and about? You don't normally surface on a weekend before midday. What's the rush?"

"Oh, well, Owen had to catch an early train so we were up..." Sonja stopped herself mid-sentence, then started again. "Wh- what I mean is, Owen was catching an early train and I wanted to see him off at the station. So I... um, got up early to say goodbye."

She looked her friend straight in the eye, daring her to comment. "I've just come from the station actually, so I thought I'd drop by to pick up my stuff."

Kerry didn't push it any further. If that was all Sonja wanted her to know, then so be it. She was well aware that everyone had their secrets; it was up to Sonja if she wanted to share them with anyone else.

Kerry smiled at her friend and decided to

change the subject. There were more pressing matters to be tackled at the moment.

"Oh, well," she said, "Ollie will be dead pleased you're here."

"Why's that?"

"Because it means you can hang around and help us tidy up."

• • •

*"Happy birthday to you...*
*Happy birthday to you...*
*Happy birthday, dear May-aaa...*
*Happy birthday to you."*

The large square table in the middle of Pizza Hut erupted into cheers as Maya stood up and graciously took a bow. She was genuinely touched that the gang had made the effort to turn out on her big day, and was even more pleased that everyone seemed to be in such high spirits. She had been worried that her birthday pizza would be a bit of an anticlimax after everyone had had such a good time last night, but the opposite seemed to be true.

"How did Nick's flat look this morning?" she asked Ollie at one point.

"Oh, like a large family of pot-bellied pigs had been on the rampage," he replied. "Fortunately,

Kerry and Sonja were there to help me clear everything up."

"Oh! Did they stay overnight then?" demanded Cat, searching desperately for a bit of gossip.

"Er, no," Ollie said, squirming in his seat. "I called them up this morning and they came over on a mission of mercy."

Ollie could have kicked himself. He'd already been sworn to secrecy by Kerry about her staying at Nick's after everyone had left.

"Hmmm, I see," Cat said, a look of total disbelief on her face. "So no juicy gossip about anyone then? How disappointing."

"I think the only gossip worth anything at all would have been if you'd got off with Andy, Cat," chuckled Ollie, expertly deferring attention from himself.

"Yeah, Cat's got more chance with that table leg than with Andy," added Matt with a smirk.

"Well, how was I to know I was the wrong sex?" Cat wailed. "No one told me."

"It would have been worth bribing Billy not to say anything to see how far you would have got," Sonja said.

Matt guffawed loudly into his pizza. "Not even past first base, I'll bet."

"I wouldn't have minded," Cat pouted, "but he never said a word."

"I reckon our Andy was having too much fun for that," replied Ollie. "He seems to be a right flirt himself. And anyway, he's so good-looking it's probably the sort of thing that happens to him all the time."

"He'll be great for The Loud," Matt enthused. "You've got to have one good-looking guy in a band or the girlies won't be interested."

"What exactly are you trying to say, Matt?" demanded Ollie, pretending to be hurt. "That the rest of us are ugly?"

"No, mate – only you. Joe and Billy are fine, but you've got to admit you let the side down a bit."

"Cheers, *mate*. Remind me not to send you free tickets when we've sold out Wembley three times over."

"Matt's just jealous because he's not in the band," Gabrielle laughed.

"He could be if he wasn't tone deaf," Ollie shot back. "And even uglier than me."

"You two are beginning to sound like Sonja and Cat, bickering away there," remarked Joe, standing up and heading towards the loos.

As he walked away from the still squabbling boys, Joe saw a beaming Kerry coming the other way. He gave her a genuinely happy smile back.

"Are you having a good time, Joe?" Kerry stopped to ask.

"Yeah, great," said Joe – and meant it.

"I've been meaning to catch you on your own to thank you for helping make Ollie and me come to our senses."

"Oh, that's OK," said Joe sheepishly, lowering his eyes. "Any time."

"No, I mean it," Kerry persisted. "It means a lot to me to know I've got friends like you looking out for me. Thank you, Joe."

Leaning forward, Kerry gave him a little kiss on the cheek. Joe felt his face catch fire at the touch of her lips, and he was sure the floor was swaying under his feet too.

Aware that she'd embarrassed him, Kerry quickly asked how things were with the band, to change the subject.

"Fabulous," Joe replied, grateful for the diversion. "It's going to be so good, Kerry, I know it. It's like I've finally found something I really want to do and it's keeping me focused. I feel really on top of it, like you wouldn't believe."

Kerry had never heard Joe so enthusiastic about anything before. It was a complete transformation. She couldn't hide her delight and grinned even wider.

"That's absolutely brilliant, Joe! I'm really pleased. You know," she went on, "I reckon this is a real turning point for you *and* for me. I think everything's going to be brilliant from now on. For both of us."

Joe reached out for Kerry's hand and held it gently in his.

"It's funny you should say that, Kerry," he said, "because I think you might be right."

# Sugar

## SECRETS...

### ...& Ambition

SNEAK PREVIEW!

"Hey, guess what!"

"What?" asked Sonja, without lifting her head from the *Yellow Pages* that she had propped open in front of her.

"Those two lads were in again!" smiled Anna conspiratorially.

Dorothy had just arrived for work and given Anna the chance to have a quick break. Since Sonja was sitting alone in the window seat with only the phone book for company, Anna had taken her orange juice and slipped into the red vinyl banquette opposite her.

"Which lads?" Sonja asked, without any real interest.

"You know! Those Dutch or Belgian boys or whatever they are. The two lads who were in here a couple of days ago!"

Sonja looked up at Anna, wrinkled her nose and shook her head.

"Nah, don't know 'em," she said flatly and dropped her gaze back down to the "M" section she was flicking through.

"Yes, you do! Really nice-looking... Kerry tripped over a backpack of theirs. Maya and me were saying how we couldn't figure out why they'd ended up in Winstead of all places..." Anna tried to jog Sonja's memory.

But Sonja either genuinely didn't remember or

she wasn't in the mood to even bother thinking about it. Anna hoped it wasn't the latter – there was nothing more infuriating than someone deliberately not getting what you were trying to say.

"Nope, sorry – don't know who you're talking about," Sonja muttered, her eyes glued downward and her finger dragging through the printed words in search of something.

Anna took a couple of calming breaths and tried to give Sonja the benefit of the doubt.

"Listen, I was thinking," she began again tentatively.

"Mmm?" muttered Sonja. Her attention wasn't wavering from the phone book.

"I bought some new stuff for my flat this weekend…"

No response.

"Nothing flash – huh, like I could afford anything flash! Just a new rug and a throw for the sofa, that kind of thing. And I just thought it would be nice to have a bit of a girls' night some time soon. What do you think?"

"Mmm," muttered Sonja again, completely missing the significance of Anna's offer.

Anna's tiny flat above the End-of-the-Line café had been her own little retreat from the world since she first moved to Winstead. Even though she'd become friends with Sonja and the others, she'd never invited them all round before.

In truth, she didn't need a retreat so much now. She'd been longing to have her new friends around for ages, but it had taken quite a while to get the place looking decent. With a mishmash of rubbishy old furniture and fittings (Nick, her landlord, had furnished it with chipped, cheap second-hand gear) and no money to do much about it, Anna had felt too embarrassed to have anyone to visit properly.

But, after a few months of bargain-hunting and hiding what she couldn't replace under remnants of Indian cloth and old tablecloths she'd dyed vivid colours, Anna finally felt she had a home she could be (almost) proud of.

All of which passed straight over Sonja's self-absorbed head.

"So, are you up for it?" asked Anna, trying to get more of a response than just "mmm".

"Yeah, yeah, your place some time. Sure. No problem," mumbled Sonja. "Ah! Here we go!"

She pulled out a small pad and pen from her bag and started scribbling.

"What have you found?" asked Anna. She realised she wouldn't get Sonja's attention today even if she tap-danced on the table and screamed that Leo DiCaprio was walking down the street.

"The name of a modelling agency up in the city."

Anna watched Sonja write a name, address and phone number down. "Is this one that Ollie's sister recommended?"

"No – she only knows agencies in London and I don't want to go that far for work. Anyway," Sonja looked up and out of the window thoughtfully, "there's something up with Tasha at the moment. I tried to talk to her about modelling when we were here on Sunday, but she just acted really bored and disinterested."

*Know the feeling...* Anna thought to herself.

"Have you heard that this agency's good then?" asked Anna, wondering how Sonja had come to choose it.

"What do you mean?" Sonja replied defensively, looking directly at Anna for only the second time since she'd sat down, and for only the first time with any real animation on her part.

"Uh, well, I just meant, does it have a good reputation?" Anna tried to explain. "You know what they're always saying in magazines: always check an agency's credentials, in case it's dodgy."

"Oh, give me some credit! It's not like I'm writing off to 'Big Boobs Incorporated' or something. I am a bit smarter than that!"

Anna felt the cold stare of Sonja's icy blue eyes

and wondered what on earth had got into her. Normally, Sonja was really good fun and always approachable.

"Well, sorry – 'course I didn't think you'd—" Anna started to apologise.

"You know something?" Sonja interrupted. "Since I mentioned this modelling thing, not *one* of my friends has had anything encouraging to say. Not Tasha, not Kerry, not Maya, and not even you."

Anna was stunned into silence by the accusation.

"If I didn't know better," said Sonja gathering up her pad and pen and shoving them into her bag, "I'd say some people round here were jealous."

Standing up, she walked away from the table and shoved the phone book back on the shelf behind the counter.

"If you'll excuse me," she said dryly to Anna as she passed by the window booth on her way to the front door, "I've got to see a boy about some photographs."

## *ARE YOU A REAL GO-GETTER?*

• • • • • • • • • • • • • • • • • • • • • • • • • •

**Do you sit around and wait to see what fate's got in store, or do you believe in making your own luck? Find out if you're the ambitious type with our quiz!**

(1) Reading about the lives of famous people in magazines is:

a) Totally inspiring – it just goes to show that anyone can do anything if they set their mind to it.

b) Totally engrossing – you love seeing how other people live.

c) Totally depressing – your life is so dull by comparison.

(2) You bump into an old friend who's just landed a dead glam new job. It makes you:

a) More determined to do something amazing with your own life.

b) Happy for them, but ever so slightly jealous at the same time.

c) Absolutely crumble with envy.

3. If your friends seem a bit half-hearted when you tell them about your plans and schemes, would you think they were:

a) Just jealous?
b) Not listening properly?
c) Like that 'cause they know you'll never get up off your couch potato bottom and do any of them?

4. If someone tells you you can't do something, do you get:

a) More determined?
b) Mad?
c) Mortified?

5. To get on you sometimes have to rely on your friends (borrowing clothes/getting lifts/getting help with homework, etc). Do you think:

a) Well, that's what friends are for?
b) It's sweet of them to help me out but it makes me feel guilty?
c) It's embarrassing having to ask them?

(6) Do you listen to lots of people's opinions before you dive in and do something?

a) No – I trust my own judgement most.

b) Yes – although I try to make up my own mind in the end.

c) Yes – even though it can make me more confused than I was in the first place.

(7) You've seen a look here, heard a dig there, and suspect your mates aren't taking you seriously. You:

a) Don't care – you know you'll have the last laugh.

b) Are irritated and decide to have a go at them about it.

c) Decide to keep quiet in future if they're going to be like that.

(8) You've made up your mind to go ahead with a plan, but keep getting niggled by doubts. Do you:

a) Carry on regardless – silly worries aren't going to put you off.

b) Mull things over till you're sure you're doing the right thing.

c) Get yourself in a right old tizz about what to do.

**(9) Believing in fate...**

a) ...is all very well, but you can't wait forever for things to happen.

b) ...is an interesting idea, but you wouldn't rely on it totally.

c) ...is essential; you can't change what's going to happen in life, so what's the point in trying?

**(10) Your motto is:**

a) "I will make it – just watch this space!"

b) "I always try to do my best – and keep my fingers crossed!"

c) "Que sera sera – what will be will be."

NOW CHECK OUT HOW YOU SCORED...

## SCORES

●●●●●●●●●●●●●●●●●●●●●●●●●●●●●●●●●●

### Mostly a

Wow – you're just like Sonja; such a go-getter that you go racing ahead, leaving everyone behind in the dust! However, Sonja's determination to get into modelling seems to blind her to everything else, and that's the flip side of having bucketloads of ambition: although you've got loads of self-confidence (brilliant), you can be mighty selfish too (most definitely *not* brilliant). Keep ploughing on with your fab ideas, but remember to make time for the important people in your life.

### Mostly b

Nobody can say that you don't have ambition, it's just that you don't always have the confidence to do anything about it! Sometimes you get held back by caution too, and that's no bad thing – in fact, it would be good if Sonja took a leaf out of your book occasionally. And you could do with a pinch of her spontaneity. Remember, your ideas are fab, so think 'em through, then put 'em into action!

### Mostly c

Ambitious? That's definitely not the first word people would come up with to describe you, but that doesn't mean you haven't got ideas. You're great at thinking things through, but you have to remember to take action too! Go on – trust your instincts; they could turn out to be right!

Coming in November 1999

# Sugar
## SECRETS...

### ...& Ambition

### GIRLS!
Matt's surrounded by them – but why
are they making him so nervous?

### TENSION!
An unexpected party guest stirs up old
resentments and sets Sonja thinking
about her future.

### AMBITION!
Sonja's aiming for The Top, but will she
have any friends left when she gets there?

*Some secrets are just too good to
keep to yourself!*

Collins
*An Imprint of* HarperCollins*Publishers*
**www.fireandwater.com**

Coming in December 1999

# Sugar
## SECRETS...
### ...& Dramas

**PARTY PARTY!**
Seems like everyone's having fun.
Everyone except Anna, that is...

**SCHEMES!**
Matt and the others are making plans –
but will their dreams come true?

**DRAMAS!**
Cat's really acting up again – and this
time she's having a ball!

*Some secrets are just too good to*
*keep to yourself!*

Collins
*An Imprint of HarperCollinsPublishers*
**www.fireandwater.com**

Coming in January 2000

# Sugar
## SECRETS...

### ...& Resolutions

**MIDNIGHT!**
Start the new year with a snog – that's
Cat's philosophy. And she's not the only
one...

**CONFUSION!**
Joe's in a muddle again. Are his feelings
for Kerry going to ruin everything?

**RESOLUTIONS!**
To tell or not to tell, that is the question.
But are they only made to be broken?

*Some secrets are just too good to
keep to yourself!*

### Collins
*An Imprint of HarperCollinsPublishers*
**www.fireandwater.com**

Coming in February 2000

# Sugar
## SECRETS...

### ...& Scandal

**VALENTINE!**
The cards predict love... but Maya
refuses to believe it.

**OBSESSION!**
Someone's got the hots for Ollie and
she's out to get him!

**SCANDAL!**
Sparks fly behind closed doors. How will
the others react when the secret's out?

*Some secrets are just too good to
keep to yourself!*

Collins
*An Imprint of HarperCollinsPublishers*
**www.fireandwater.com**

# Sugar
## *SECRETS...*

### *...& Revenge*

**LOVE!**
Cat's in love with the oh-so-gorgeous
Matt and don't her friends know it.

**HUMILIATION!**
Then he's caught snogging Someone
Else at Ollie's party.

**REVENGE!**
Watch out Matt – Cat's claws are out...

Meet the whole crowd in the first ever
episode of Sugar Secrets.

*Some secrets are just too good to
keep to yourself!*

## Collins
*An Imprint of HarperCollinsPublishers*
**www.fireandwater.com**

# Sugar
## SECRETS...
### ...& Lies

**CONFESSIONS!**
Is Ollie in love? Yes? No? Definitely
maybe!

**THE TRUTH!**
Sonja is determined to find out who the
lucky girl can be.

**LIES!**
But someone's not being honest, which
might just break Kerry's heart...

*Some secrets are just too good to
keep to yourself!*

### Collins
*An Imprint of HarperCollinsPublishers*
**www.fireandwater.com**

# Sugar
## SECRETS...

### ...& Lust

**DATE-DEPRIVATION!**
Sonja laments the lack of fanciable
blokes around, then two come along at
once.

**MYSTERY STRANGER!**
One is seriously cute, but why is he
looking for Anna?

**LUST!**
Will Sonja choose Kyle or Owen –
or both?!

*Some secrets are just too good to*
*keep to yourself!*

Collins
*An Imprint of HarperCollinsPublishers*
**www.fireandwater.com**

# Order Form

To order direct from the publishers, just make a list of the titles you want and fill in the form below:

Name .................................................................................

Address ...........................................................................

..........................................................................................

..........................................................................................

Send to: Dept 6, HarperCollins Publishers Ltd, Westerhill Road, Bishopbriggs, Glasgow G64 2QT.

Please enclose a cheque or postal order to the value of the cover price, plus:

UK & BFPO: Add £1.00 for the first book, and 25p per copy for each additional book ordered.

Overseas and Eire: Add £2.95 service charge. Books will be sent by surface mail but quotes for airmail despatch will be given on request.

A 24-hour telephone ordering service is available to Visa and Access card holders: 0141- 772 2281

Collins
An *Imprint* of HarperCollins*Publishers*